1966

WOULD YOU
BELIEVE...

- A better mousetrap making a crucial difference in the winning of the race to conquer outer space?
- Steve "The Man from O.R.G.Y." Victor getting married?
- A beautiful female campaigner for clean literature wearing a startling bikini?
- Steve "The Man from—!" being pursued and shot at by Russians, Americans, and strictly free-lance spies?

It's all here . . . with much more . . . in Ted Mark's latest laugh-and-action espionage thriller!

A Hard Day's Knight

TED MARK

LANCER BOOKS • NEW YORK

A LANCER BOOK • 1966

A HARD DAY'S KNIGHT

LANCER BOOKS, INC. • 185 MADISON AVENUE • NEW YORK, N.Y. 10016

chapter
ONE

MY FIRST EVENING in Washington, D. C., was a lonely one. I thought about calling the Johnsons, but decided against it. Texas hospitality is renowned, but it wouldn't have been fair to call even so gracious a hostess as Lady Bird at the last minute that way. And much as I admired Lyndon, I didn't really want to spend an evening listening to him justify his Vietnam policies—a topic of conversation which seemed to have become somewhat compulsive with him lately. Besides, to be honest about it, while my status as a taxpayer might entitle me to take potluck at the White House, I'm not what you'd call really close with the President and his lady. The truth is that while I voted for him, we've never really met. So I dined alone.

After dinner I killed time by taking a stroll through Rock Creek Park. I wasn't due to meet Charles Putnam until after one a. m. and there was nothing to keep me hanging around my hotel. The Windsor was a very nice, quietly plush hostelry, but too conservative for my taste, and definitely not where the action was. Putnam wasn't staying there himself. Why had he insisted on booking me a room there?

I didn't know the answer. But then there were lots of answers I didn't know where Charles Putnam was concerned. For instance, where had he gone after leaving me at the airport when we disembarked from the unmarked and exclusive government plane which had ferried us from Manila? Where was he right now?

The other side of the Looking-Glass—that was my guess. Holding hands with Alice and sure-footedly picking his way through the Washington wonderland of cloak-and-dagger diplomacy. Yes, I could picture him holding whispered conversations with the White Knight and the Red Queen. I could see him sipping exotic LSD tea with Haigha and Hatta and bouncing the world like a rubber ball as he wended his way back to the Looking-glass exit.

The fantasy suited my opinion of Putnam. Experience had taught me never to take his reality for granted. Even his name, he'd admitted to me once, was an invented monicker. Add a face out of Grimm's Fairy Tales, a physique that was Herculean, an impeccable manner and style of dress worthy of C. Aubrey Smith looking down his nose at the Student Prince, and you get a picture of the contradictory character I couldn't quite believe in even when I was face to face with him.

Such occasions added to the feeling of his unreality by reminding me of his nebulous—but extremely important—status in the world of undercover government activity. Charles Putnam had something to do with the State Department, but officially the State Department had never heard of him. He also had something to do with the CIA, but the CIA wouldn't even acknowledge his existence. He floated in that murky void between diplomacy and espionage, the void encompassing the Bay of Pigs and unofficial confabs with the Red Chinese, U-2 flights, and quiet, preliminary talks on disarmament points which might be discussed, containment and co-existence. Yes, somewhere between containment and co-existence, Putnam could be found patriotically zigzagging along the course of U. S. foreign policy and frequently, I suspected, proving instrumental in formulating it.

While there might be some doubt about whether Putnam was a pawn, or a player, or both, in my own case there was no doubt whatsoever. I was a pawn—Putnam's pawn—a pawn made willing (if not eager) to be moved about at Putnam's whim by my own strong feelings of patriotism. Don't get me wrong. I'm no flag-waver. But, considering the alternatives, I guess I buy the "My country, may she always be right, but right or wrong, etc." philosophy. Many's the governmental madness I deplore, but they haven't yet contrived a Utopia I'd consider swapping for the U. S.

That's my simple reason for letting myself be used by Putnam. His reason for finding me useful stems from my unique line of work. You see, I'm Steve Victor, the man from O. R. G. Y.

Let me explain. O. R. G. Y. is the Organization for the Rational Guidance of Youth. Some people might consider that mouthful a misnomer, but I'm not one of them. The reason that they might cock a skeptical eybrow at the name is that the real work of O. R. G. Y. is sex research. It's a one-man foundation—the one man being me—which often receives grants for research from wealthier foundations. In exchange for these moneys, O. R. G. Y. conducts surveys and compiles statistics on many aspects of sex in many parts of the world. These statistics, as I see it, often are used for the rational guidance of youth. And they can use whatever rational guidance they can get in today's mixed up world of sex.

Once, O. R. G. Y. was not only my means of earning a livelihood, but also my prime concern. Since meeting Charles Putnam, that is no longer true. He'd decided my experience and knowledge of the nether worlds of sex could be invaluable to him and therefore to our government. So he'd enlisted me for one adventure after another by appealing to my patriotism. This time he'd practically drafted me, dragging me off from Manila to Washington on short notice and parking me without any explanation save that he'd give me one at our next meeting.

That next meeting was still two hours off, but I'd had enough of the park. It was depressing, strolling about all by myself among the entwined couples on the benches. The sounds of their sighs in the breeze only seemed to increase my feeling of loneliness. I headed back to the Windsor and went up to my room.

Without intending to, I sacked out. A low knocking at the door woke me. I admitted Charles Putnam. "Well, what's up?" I greeted him as he carefully closed and locked the door behind himself.

"It seems that your government has need of your unique talents again, Mr. Victor. All I knew in Manila was that my instructions were to bring you back to Washington with me. Now I know why."

"So let me in on the secret."

"I shall. And it is a secret. Let me caution you about that. What I have to tell you is top secret, hush-hush."

"I'll pass the word along to my vocal cords," I promised. "Now what say you get down to the nitty-gritty?"

"Very well. About a week ago a man walked into the U. S. Patent Office here in Washington. He had a small invention with him, a gadget, but no blueprints. When the clerk in charge told him he'd have to present plans as well as the invention itself in order to obtain a patent, he became very annoyed. He became loud and made several derogatory statements about bureaucratic red tape."

"Did they throw him out?"

"No. He left under his own steam. But not before he'd managed to antagonize most of the personnel and draw a

8

great deal of attention to himself. Anyway, after leaving the Patent Office, as well as we've been able to determine, he stopped off in a bakery in the neighborhood and purchased a loaf of stale bread."

"Why stale bread?"

"You'll see. I'm coming to that in a minute. Anyway, the bakery proprietor remembers him for two reasons. The first was his insistence that the bread be really stale enough. The second was the fact that while he was standing there waiting for the proprietor to get through serving other customers, the man kept muttering insulting things about the Patent Office."

"He hadn't cooled down yet," I summed up.

"Exactly. To continue, from the bake shop he took a bus to Rock Creek Park. Here he spent about an hour studying various birds through field glasses and making notes in a small notebook. Then he sat down on a park bench and crumbled up the stale bread. This done, he began feeding the birds with the bread crumbs."

"Bread crumbs?"

"Bread crumbs."

"I see. But how do you know all this?" I wanted to know. "Did you have the man under surveillance?"

"No. But his bird-watching activities attracted the attention of another man who was passing the time of day sunning himself on a park bench. This second man was later bemused by the birds scrambling for the bread crumbs. He strolled over to the bench where the first man was feeding them and struck up a conversation with him."

"First man, second man—I'm getting confused," I told Putnam. "Don't these people have names?"

"Yes. The first man, the inventor, has been identified as one Anthony Bowdler Cromwell. Is that name familiar to you, Mr. Victor?" Putnam added as he noted the flicker of recognition which crossed my face.

9

"It is," I nodded, struggling to remember why it should be. "But I'm not quite sure in what context at the moment. Go on with your story."

"Try to recall where you know the name from; it could be important. Meanwhile, I'll continue. Where was I? Ah yes, names. Well, the second man, the one who'd been idly watching Cromwell and then fell into conversation with him, as Knute Hajstrom. He's an aeronautical engineer on loan to the U. S. government space program from a university in Sweden. One of the top men in his field, he's an integral part of our long-range project to put a man on the moon. He's currently in Washington for top-level conferences at the Pentagon. This particular day in the park, he was killing time between two such conferences."

"What's all that got to do with our bread-crumby friend?"

"Quite a lot, Mr. Victor, as you shall see. After a while, Cromwell began griping to Hajstrom about the treatment he'd received at the Patent Office. Hajstrom is a very kindly man. He figured Cromwell for some kind of a nut, but he listened anyway. However, when Cromwell showed him the gadget itself, Hajstrom revised his opinion in a hurry."

"Don't tell me; let me guess. This do-it-yourself putterer invented a moon rocket in his own backyard workshop."

"No. But in a vague way you're on the right track. The actual gadget he'd been trying to patent was of very doubtful worth, but—"

"Then how am I on the right track?" I wanted to know. "And what was the gadget?"

"A mousetrap."

"A mousetrap?"

"A mousetrap!"

"You've got to be kidding."

"I am not kidding," Putnam assured me. "Cromwell had invented a mousetrap."

"A better mousetrap?" I asked.

"I'm in no position to judge that."

"I was just trying to determine if the world was beating a path to his door," I apologized.

"Somebody beat a path to his door and made off with the cheese." Putnam smiled drily. "But I'm getting ahead of my story. What excited Hajstrom's interest was not the mousetrap itself, but what had been done to the material of which it was made."

"What was it made of?"

"Aluminum. But no ordinary aluminum. This aluminum was harder than steel. Also, it had more resistance to heat. Cromwell had evidently developed some completely new process for tempering it. That process, in Hajstrom's judgment, could chop ten years off the time needed to put us on the moon if we had it. The resistance of the metal Cromwell showed him makes it ideal for space travel."

"How could Hajstrom tell all this from just looking at the thing?"

"For one thing, the use of metal alloys in space is his particular specialty. For another, he was able to evaluate its qualities from observing the difficulty Cromwell had in trying to destroy it."

"Destroy it? Why should he do that?"

"Evidently Cromwell was really playing the dog in the manger. The more he told Hajstrom about his experiences with government bureaucracy, the madder he got. Finally he said the devil with the whole thing, if nobody appreciated his invention he was going to destroy it and leave Washington and go back where he came from. Hajstrom tried to dissuade him, but it was no use. By then Cromwell was all but frothing at the mouth."

"How did he destroy it?"

"It wasn't easy. He picked up a loose brick and tried to pound the mousetrap to bits. It was no use. The brick crumbled; the mousetrap was intact. Then he tried to set fire to it with his cigarette lighter. It wouldn't burn. Finally he walked over to the lake with Hajstrom beside him and still trying to talk him out of it. But it was no use. Cromwell flung the thing as far out as he could, and it sank."

"If it's as important as you say it is, why not drag the lake for the mousetrap?"

"We're doing that. But the chances of recovering it are slim. The lake has a strong undercurrent. This comes from a deep underground stream. Once the mousetrap is sucked into it, the chances are against our ever finding it. And then there's some question as to just how much use it would be to us if we did find it."

"What do you mean?" I asked.

"It's Hajstrom's feelng that even if we had the object we might never be able to determine the process by which the alloy was developed."

"Why not simply ask Cromwell?"

"Brilliant, Mr. Victor!" There was grating sarcasm in the way Putnam said it. "There's only one trouble. Cromwell has disappeared."

"Oh?"

"Yes. After throwing the mousetrap in the lake, he parted company with Hajstrom. He said he was going back to his hotel. When Hajstrom said he might want to reach him, Cromwell told him he was staying at the Windsor. Hajstrom went straight to the Pentagon and told certain very important people about the qualities of the metal Cromwell had shown him. It was decided to send for Cromwell immediately. It was about ten at night when an agent from the Pentagon arrived at Cromwell's rooms. Cromwell wasn't there. And he hasn't been back

12

since. That was a week ago. It's as if the earth had swallowed him up."

"He didn't check out of the hotel?"

"No. The desk clerk saw him come in at about five o'clock—which fits in with the time he left Hajstrom. There were a few incoming phone calls between then and eight-thirty, when he and his wife were seen leaving the hotel together. However, there were no outgoing calls made."

"His wife? Where is she?"

"Presumably with him. She never returned, either."

"I presume you've checked out Cromwell's background?"

"Yes. The FBI was put on that even before I was contacted in Manila. Not much there. Anthony Bowdler Cromwell, age thirty years"—Putnam was rattling it off from a small photostat he'd taken from his pocket—"born and raised in Danville, Indiana, grade and high school educations there, also graduated Central Normal College in Danville. Since his graduation, he has been employed as a statistician and cost accountant in a local foundry. Two promotions with raises and he's in line for a third. His boss rates him extremely competent and conscientious. Neither his boss nor fellow employees were aware that he was an amateur inventor. Some of his neighbors know because he converted his garage into a workshop and always leaves his car parked in the driveway. But they have no idea what he was working on. He's been married six years. His wife is twenty-six years of age, name Carrie Cromwell, nee Carrie Semple."

"That's it!" I snapped my fingers. "Now I remember! She's a gingham type with an aprony manner that's supposed to make you forget the way her hips wiggle and the 39-inch bosom she points in your face. Sure, one of those respiratory systems that's always heaving with vir-

13

tue like a canary trying to get out of its cage. Nice legs with dimpled knees and hot thighs that always managed to sneak out from under those demure long skirts she wore. Wholesome brown hair with a wholesome curl and wholesome bangs and a wholesome face under it, a face so sincere it made you want to run right out and buy a copy of *Good Housekeeping*, but with a sort of smoldering in the brown eyes that made you wonder about the wholesomeness and the sincerity. Carrie Cromwell—I remember her well."

"It does sound like she made quite an impression on you," Putnam observed.

"She did. It's been at least five years, and I only met her the one time. But the contrast between the morality she was spouting then and the sexy way she looked stuck in my mind."

"Well"—Putnam consulted his photostats—"the description you give would seem to tally with the one we have of her. What about her husband? Did you meet him?"

"Sure."

"Can you describe him?"

"Roughly my height, just over six feet. Wispy blond hair, light blue eyes a little on the watery side, skinny, with narrow shoulders and a thin, sort of ascetic face. A good, deep voice, though—I remember that—and a delivery that might strike some people as impressive and others as ponderous and pompous. A logical mind, the kind that ticks off points—one-two-three, you know—and a very pedantic, very black-and-white approach to things. But of course I could be biased about that."

"Why 'of course,' Mr. Victor?"

"Because of the circumstances of our meeting. It was a debate, a sort of public forum, and we were on opposite sides."

"What was the topic?"

14

"*Resolved: Moral Laxity is Destroying the Fabric of Modern Society in America Today.* He took the affirmative. I took the negative. I'd been asked to debate because of my connection with O. R. G. Y. and because I'd studied under Kinsey at Indiana U while he was still alive. Cromwell, as I recall, was the present of some state-wide group devoted to outlawing so-called pornography. The debate took place in Bloomington. Not at the University, though. It was sponsored by some sort of civic organization and held in a public hall. His wife was up on the platform with him. After the discussion, she sort of launched a private offensive against me personally. She was prissy as hell, but she was also damn attractive, so I kept the argument going even when it was obvious that her husband was annoyed and wanted to leave. I remember they hadn't been married too long then and I twitted her about not really having the experience to discuss lapses in morality. She laughed and looked interested; at that point Cromwell did drag her away."

"It's a stroke of luck that you know them, Mr. Victor. Now I'm sure that you're the man to track them down."

"You say they've both been missing for a week?"

"Yes."

I pondered that one for a moment. Then I posed another question. "But somebody wanted me on the job even before you knew I'd met them. Why? Why me?"

"Because of two very small clues which may give the only hints to their whereabouts."

"What clues?"

"I think it would be best if you saw them for yourself," Putnam said firmly. "Their quarters have been gone over by government agents with a fine-tooth comb, but it was done so that everything was left exactly as it was when the Cromwells departed. It's two floors below this one. Come along and I'll show you."

Putnam led the way out the door and down the hallway to the staircase. We walked down two flights and stopped in front of the door directly in front of the stairway exit. Putnam took out a key and opened it. He motioned for me to precede him into the room.

At first glance it seemed the ordinary sort of scene you'd expect in a hotel room. Two suitcases on the floor in front of the window: one opened, one closed. There was some men's underwear and socks visible in the opened one. One of the closets was also opened, and there were three rather conservative dresses hanging in it. The bathroom door was ajar, and there were toiletries on the shelf over the sink. The bed was made, but the spread was ruffled as if someone had been lying on top of it. I took a second look at the spread and immediately spotted the first of the clues Putnam had mentioned.

It was a pair of women's panties, cut bikini style, and made of leather! I picked them up and looked at Putnam quizzically. "You ran a trace on these, I presume," I said.

"Yes. But it was a dead end. They're homemade. No label. And the leather is common. It could have come from anywhere."

"What about the styling?"

"It's common in bathing suits, and even in women's lingerie today."

"Yeah," I agreed. I held the panties up and eyed them and tried to remember. "They'd fit Carrie Cromwell," I said tentatively.

"From the descriptions we've obtained of her, there's no doubt they would."

"My first impulse is to say it's out of character," I told him, "but I wonder . . ."

"Take another look around, and perhaps you'll see something to make you wonder even more."

I did, and finally I spotted the tabloid on the night table. It was one of those irregularly published magazines with

16

a newspaper format. You know the kind—attention-getting headlines like "I WAS RAPED BY MY TOY BULLDOG" or "CONFESSIONS OF A BABY-KILLER" or "WHY THE NINTH POSITION MADE ME HAPPIEST" (by some allegedly nymphomaniac, but probably really frigid, female movie star) all in 48-point type over stories in cheap, blurry newsprint with even murkier photos to illustrate them. The last eight pages of this one were devoted to the personal ad columns. The paper had been folded back to one of these pages, and one of the ads had been circled. I picked it up and read it to myself.

"SEX MUST BE DISCIPLINED"—that was the heading. And underneath—"Young married couple devoted to spreading Prussian rules of sexual behavior eager to contact other young marrieds with similar viewpoint." A Washington, D. C., box number followed the ad copy.

"Did they check out the box number?" I asked Putnam.

"Yes. It's the mail drop for a bookstore proprietor. Evidently he picks it up and re-distributes it himself."

"Did they sweat him?"

"No. He's under surveillance, but he hasn't been picked up. The feeling was that if he was grabbed it would be like sounding the alarm for those involved with him. That might wash out the Cromwells' trail altogether. Whatever they've gotten themselves involved in, it's far more important that Cromwell be found than that we crack down on some sort of vice setup. That's where you come in. Your job is to find out just what the setup is, infiltrate it any way you can, and find Cromwell. That's why they had me bring you to Washington. You're the only man with the requisite experience in both the vice world and undercover work that's needed in this case."

"Okay," I sighed. "Give me the name of the bookseller. I'll get started in the morning."

Putnam walked me back up to my own room, gave me the information, and then left. I got undressed and went to bed. I lay awake for a while, staring at the ceiling and thinking of Carrie Cromwell and leather panties. Finally the visions merged and I drifted into a dream.

There was Carrie stepping out of a calfskin nightgown, her breasts panting yes, her brown curls swirling as her head shook no-no-no. I reached for her, and her lips turned to leather. I backed away, and she was all flesh again. But now she was sharpening a hatpin on a leather strop, the kind barbers use to hone razors. I shrugged resignedly, and immediately she threw her arms around me. I noticed a "Made In Marriage Only" stamp on her shoulder. I forgot about it when she began moaning for me to hurry up. I threw her down on a bed, and she went wild. Then, suddenly, there was a sharp crack like the sound of a leather belt being snapped . . .

The sound woke me. I opened my eyes on the darkened hotel room, and they tried to ferret out the cause of it. They peered toward a bureau across the room. My ears re-evaluated the sound and decided it could have been caused by the inadvertent slamming of a bureau drawer which had been stuck. My eyes saw the silhouette of a figure in front of the bureau now and confirmed the guess. My brain, still half asleep, reacted stupidly.

"Hey! What the hell—?" I started to yell.

The figure was a quick-moving blur that ended up hovering over me. I had a quick look at the face before my eyes were closed again. It was like looking into a mirror. It was my face. I blinked, and then it was too late for another look. Something very heavy hit me very hard on the head.

I dived down into a tunnel of black mirrors. There were reflections inside reflections inside reflections, and they were all me. They continued on into pitch-dark infinity. Yet I kept plunging, chasing them until they grew smaller and smaller and smaller until I was chasing only the most infinitesimal dot of a Steve Victor.

The dot hurt like hell. Even after it vanished and there was nothing but the black void, it kept on hurting. Now black agony was all there was.

No dream. No Carrie Cromwell. No leather panties, even. Just black pain filling my skull!

chapter
TWO

THE MORNING SUN didn't wake me from sleep; it just blazed bright enough finally to jar me back to consciousness. I swam back up through the mirrors with their repeating images and pried up the lids over my aching eyeballs. Now, instead of the repetitious me, I was seeing that ball of fire poking fingers of light through the window and into my sensitive orbs.

I cringed and turned away from the sunshine. As if I hadn't had enough of mirrored nightmares, I got out of bed and crossed over to the mirror over the bureau to see if the real Steve Victor was still in condition to stand up. Barely. That's what the mirror told me. There was a lump on the side of my head the size of a shot glass. The mirror didn't have to tell me that, though. I got the message direct from the way it was throbbing.

Hobbling back over to the telephone on the night table, I called room service. I told them to send up a pot of black coffee and a bucket of ice. The party on the other end misunderstood.

"Do you want iced coffee, sir?" he asked, confused.

"No. I prefer to make it myself," I said nastily, taking

out my headache on him. "Just send up the hot coffee in a pot and the ice in a bucket."

"Very well, sir." The voice was unperturbed by my rudeness.

While I was waiting, I surveyed the room. Evidently, once he'd been spotted, the intruder hadn't bothered to cover up the traces of the ransacking he'd given the place. The clothes which had been in my suitcase were on the floor where he'd flung them. One of the bureau drawers was still open. The trousers I'd hung in the closet had been tossed on a chair. They lay there with the pockets turned inside-out.

My wallet had been inside one of those pockets. It was gone. Besides various identification papers and about fifty bucks in cash, the slip of paper with the address and name of the bookseller on it which Putnam had given me was in the wallet. So now the intruder with my face had the papers to back it up and the signpost pointing to Cromwell's trail—if that was where his interest lay.

Was it? I thought about it. Everything had happened so fast the night before that it was hard for me to be sure where dream-fantasy had ended and reality had begun. Nor was I sure where reality had ceased and hallucination might have started me down the road to unconsciousness.

Had the intruder really been a ringer for me? Or had I imagined it? The question was crucial!

It was crucial because if I hadn't been hallucinating, that double meant trouble. Real serious trouble! There was only one other man in the world that I knew of with my face. He hadn't been born with it. It had deliberately been grafted on him. And that man was a Russian agent who'd whimsically assigned himself the name of Viktor Stevkovsky.

Stevkovsky and I had crossed paths violently in Manila. My assumption was that I'd left him behind there. But if

21

I hadn't, if he was in Washington, if it really had been him in my room last night, then I could look foward to hard times acomin'. If Stevkovsky was dogging me again, then it meant the Russians knew about Cromwell's process and were after it.

Still, I had to admit to myself that my mind could have played tricks on me. I had a grudge against Stevkovsky that transcended opposing political philosophies and had kept him in the forefront of my mind since Manila. The grudge had to do with a girl Stevkovsky had seduced by pretending to be me. Even in the capers of agents, double agents, double crosses and triple plays, some things are inexcusable. And bedding down my girl by impersonating me is one of them. So I'd had many smoldering thoughts about Stevkovsky, and it was possible that in my semi-sleep my brain might have imposed his features— my features, that is—on the intruder.

It was a possibility, but not the one on which I could afford to act. Even if I'd dreamed it up, I had to assume that Stevkovsky was the intruder and that he'd turn up again. That meant that certain precautions were needed. I picked up the telephone and called Putnam to arrange them.

"I think you may have sprung a leak," I told him when he answered the phone.

"I beg your pardon?"

"Nothing personal. I mean a security leak. I have reason to think the Russians may be on to the Cromwell case."

"Explain," he said curtly.

I did. "So watch out for somebody impersonating me," I concluded. "Even if it's face to face, make damn sure it's me. We'd better have a code word so I can identify myself. 'American original'," I decided on the spur of the moment. "I'll always use that phrase for positive identification. If a Steve Victor turns up who doesn't say that, lock him up and throw the key away."

22

" 'American original'," Putnam repeated. "Very well."

I got the name and address of the bookseller from him again and hung up the phone. A waiter knocked at the door just as the conversation ended. I took the tray with the coffee and the bucket of ice on it from him. I gulped the coffee, and it steamed its way down to my stomach. I wrapped the ice in a towel and put my head in deep freeze for about twenty minutes.

It left me feeling a helluva lot better. A hot shower finished the job. I still had a dull headache, but it was possible to ignore it as I got dressed. I went downstairs, hailed a taxi, and gave him the address of the book store.

When we got into the neighborhood, I had the driver drop me at the corner of U Street and Fourteenth Street. I didn't want to get out of the cab in front of my destination. I didn't want to look that prosperous. And I didn't want my visit to look that deliberate.

After I got out, I walked down U Street toward Eleventh. It's a sort of a quiet Times Square-ish area. There's none of the real honky-tonk found on New York's 42nd Street, but the same sort of establishments line the block. The storefront windows are filled with bargain-basement garments—all advertised as on sale— and cheap souvenirs. Each block along U Street has its quota of bars and deep-frying pizza and hamburger joints. There are a lot of hole-in-the-wall book shops in the area, and only the address I had helped me distinguish my destination from any of the others. I stood casually outside and studied the small shop for a moment.

It was called The Velvet Book Mart. The name of the proprietor, which I'd gotten from Putnam, was Martin Velvet. The names might or might not be meaningful.

There was nothing velvet-y about him. Martin Velvet was a small, thin man of indeterminate age with the sharp ferret features of a pool-hall hustler. Both eyes were beady, and one was permanently squinted as if conditioned by hours of sighting down the shaft of a cue stick. His nose was long and straight, designed for looking down to line up a carom shot. And his voice, least velvet-y of all, was like a megaphoned version of the squeaky, grating sound made by a nervous player over-chalking his cue stick before a particularly difficult shot.

"Looking for something special?" The grinding rasp greeted me as I entered the bookstore.

He'd given me a good opening. I took advantage of it. "Yeah," I told him. "A friend of mine told me to drop in here when I hit Washington. He said you handled the sort of stuff that might appeal to a very sophisticated mixed group."

Window shades came down over both eyes. Velvet peeked out from under them with a look that managed to be furtive and suspicious and knowing and afraid all at the same time. "Who was the friend?" he asked.

"A disciplinarian," I told him, using underground parlance for a sex sadist. "I'd rather not mention his name."

"How do I know you ain't a cop?" Velvet asked.

"You don't. But maybe a hundred bucks might make you willing to chance it."

"Just a first name and an address. That's all the C-note buys. After that I don't know anything. I don't want to know anything."

"Okay. As long as they're real swingers," I said pointedly.

"I wouldn't know that, either. Maybe we mean two different things by 'swingers.' Maybe I just mean they're congenial, friendly, hospitable couples who like to make new acquaintances. You take your chances. That's all a C-note buys."

"What would another fifty buy?"

"Not much. A little innocent information, maybe."

I handed him a hundred and fifty and waited.

24

"George and Helen," he said, mentioning an address after the names.

"And for the fifty?" I reminded him.

"They're interested in French culture."

"How interested?"

"They speak the language very well. They're both cunning linguists."

"Do they play any instruments?"

"The French horn."

In essence, this cryptic exchange had told me by use of the code words common to members of the sex underground that George and Helen were a couple who engaged in oral sex with partners of either gender. This wasn't quite the lead I was seeking, but my experience told me that any entry into this nether world was worthwhile. The groups engaging in various specialized activities are usually interlocking, and members frequently belong to two or three of them, or at least have knowledge of the activities of the others. Still, I made a try for a direct approach. "Would another fifty buy me some German drill instruction?" I asked Velvet.

"Not even another hundred," he said firmly. "Don't you read the papers? They're really cracking down on the Huns. That big case in Jersey recently pointed the finger at a lot of Prussians around the country."

"There must be some discipline," I said pointedly.

"Nope. People are even afraid to spank their kids any more."

"Tell me more about George and Helen," I suggested.

"Nope. I said too much already. I don't even know them personally. All I know is I hear they're real hospitable to married couples with the same interests they have."

"Couples?" That brought me up short. "What about bachelors?"

"Nix. Strictly young marrieds. They like to keep everything even. They don't want any squares and they figure you have to be married to be sophisticated enough for them. If you're not married—" He shrugged and tucked the hundred and fifty more snugly into his pocket.

"I am," I assured him.

"Then I'll see that they expect you, uh—?"

I realized he wanted a name and he didn't much care if it was a real name or not. "Steve," I told him.

"Okay, Steve. Drop around again sometime." He said it in a way that left no doubt the interview was over.

I left figuring that he'd be on the wire to George and Helen as soon as I was out the door. Probably he had some sort of deal with them for steering "swingers" their way. I didn't give it too much thought. There was something else bugging me. And it was something I had to solve before dropping in on George and Helen. The problem was—

Since I was going to join a wife-swapping club, where was I going to get a wife to swap?

chapter
THREE

I RECRUITED HER. Or maybe, drafted would be a better description. Yep, I drafted me an ever-lovin' wife from right out of the eagerly waiting arms of a select group of U. S. congressmen. And I had to beat out a mighty powerful lobby to do it.

To explain— My make-believe Mrs. Victor was really an upper-bracket call girl named Hortense—last name deliberately lost to posterity. Hortense was one of a particular group of such ladies of the night whose services were pretty much monopolized by an important firm of lobbyists. Persuasion being the profession of these lobbyists, they had found that when it came to persuading legislators to vote the way they wanted them to, Hortense and her sisters were unsurpassed. Indeed, the persuasive powers of these girls was so potent that when lesser play-for-pay lassies were fleeing Washington in the wake of the Bobby Baker contretemps, they not only kept on working steadily, but even aided in softening the harsh judgments of some of the policy-makers who were publicly the most outraged by Baker's tart.

The day that I contacted her, Hortense was scheduled

for some intimate and private congressional investigation. Her lobbyist employers had selected her personally to make a committee head see the light. It wasn't easy to convince her that my needs took precedence.

If it hadn't been for the fact that I'd known Hortense for some time, and that she owed me a favor, I doubt that I could even have talked her into coming up to my hotel room to discuss what I had in mind. I'd first met her a few years back when I was doing an O. R. G. Y. survey on the experiences of hundred-dollar-a-night-and-up call girls. How I'd managed to have pressure brought to bear on her and other girls to cooperate is a long story. Suffice it to say that Hortense did cooperate. Then, when I was further along with the survey, we both found ourselves at the same "party" one night. The affair was raided. It happened that I had some connections in the particular city where this occurred. As soon as I identified myself, I was released on the grounds that I was a social scientist doing research work. If the cop who signed me out of the calaboose smirked at the designation, it was nothing to the dirty look he gave me when I insisted that Hortense was my assistant and arranged for her release as well. I did it on the spur of the moment and only because she'd been so pleasant when I interviewed her. Her appreciation had taken the form of writing me a few months later to tell me she was "working" in Washington. She enclosed a phone number so I could call her if ever I was in town.

So I called Hortense. She told me she was sorry but she was tied up, and explained why. But I told her it was urgent without explaining why and finally got her to agree to come and talk to me. It was about an hour after I hung up the phone that I heard her knocking lightly at the door.

"Is that Hortense?" I called out.

"Yes."

"Well, relax—and come on in."

She entered. She hadn't changed. She'd looked about eighteen when I first met her, and she still looked about eighteen, although she must be in her mid-twenties by now. She was still a beautiful girl with the kind of allure that's almost startling.

Her hair was a dark red chestnut color with a sheen that caught the light no matter which way she turned. It reached to her shoulders, and she wore it simply, parted in the middle and brushed so that it rippled gently as it occasionally grazed her cheeks. It provided a sort of halo-like framing for the slightly feline and very sensual face it outlined.

The face too was compelling, the eyes most of all. They were a very dark green flecked ever so lightly with gold, and they slanted slightly, like a cat's eyes. And like a cat, Hortense rarely blinked; once a man encountered this direct gaze, it was difficult to relinquish it. Fathoming it was a challenge, and the challenge of Hortense's eyes was ever mysterious and feminine.

Her high cheekbones accentuated this impression. But her nose, just a bit upturned, and her mouth, set off by dimples and seeming always to be on the verge of laughing, relieved it. If her eyes and cheekbones were catlike, her mouth and nose were kittenish, more playful, more promising of fun than unrelieved sensuality.

Taking the optic elevator down the structure of Hortense's figure, though, sensuality again reigned supreme. This, despite the fact that the dark green knit dress she was wearing covered most of her charms quite demurely. Not quite so demure was the way the dress clung to her large, torpedo-shaped breasts and well-rounded hips. It stretched tight over a very provocative *derriere*, and it was short enough so that when she sat down a good deal of her beauty-contest legs was revealed. She was a tall girl, and the overall impression was one of her being slender and voluptuous at the same time. She wouldn't have looked out of place with the near-Amazons of the Copacabana chorus line.

Hortense was sexy-looking, but she also had a great deal of poise, and despite her profession she was never obvious in the way she handled herself. Personality-wise, she was like a fun-loving coed from an upper-bracket college: attentive, quick to laughter, but with just enough restraint so that she always maintained a certain dignity. She was the kind of girl you could take anywhere and be sure that her quiet style would never embarrass you.

I told Hortense that I was doing another survey for O. R. G. Y. and that I needed her help. I explained that this one had to do with various types of sex clubs involving young marrieds, most of which entailed some ritualistic form of wife-swapping. Needing a wife to swap, I said, it occurred to me that Hortense would be just the girl to pose as my mate for as long as the survey might take.

Hortense said she'd like to help me out, but I'd picked a bad time. She explained about being booked up by the lobby to "entertain" the congressmen. There was an obligation not to let them down, and also one to herself, since it would bring her in a great deal of money over a relatively short time.

"If you'll agree to go along with me, I can take care of both your objections," I promised her.

"What do you mean?"

"I'll see that you're paid whatever you might have made. And I'll make sure that you're voluntarily released from your other assignment without prejudice to your future career."

"If you can do that, Steve, I'd be happy to help you out."

"Leave it to me. You go rest up for what's left of the afternoon. Come back here about nine tonight and everything will have been arranged."

"Okay. I trust you, Steve. I won't even ask how you can do it." She got to her feet. "I'll see you later, then."

When the door closed behind her, I got on the horn to Putnam. He didn't question the money I told him I'd need to pay Hortense for her time. And he said it would be no problem to apply the pressure needed to get her released from her congressional assignment. That settled, I asked him to run a fast check on George and Helen, gave him the address Velvet had provided, and hung up on Putnam's promise that he'd get back to me at eight-thirty that evening.

Putnam was as good as his word. His return call at eight-thirty didn't provide any world-shaking information, but then given the time alloted I'd known the check would have to be superficial and hadn't expected that it would. Still, after I hung up on Putnam, I committed to memory the notes I'd made on what he'd told me, figuring they might or might not come in handy later on in the evening.

Their last name was Quentin. They'd been married five years. George Quentin was a lawyer employed by a large corporation which manufactured precision optical equipment. He was in Washington to handle the legal work connected with the bidding on and renewal of contracts his firm had with the Pentagon. His salary was $30,000 per year, which was pretty good for a twenty-nine-year-old barrister, even if he was a Yale graduate.

His wife, Helen, was three years younger than George. She'd graduated *summa cum laude* from Vassar. Originally she was from Philadelphia where her family was well-known and ultra-respectable without being particularly wealthy. She'd met George, who was from New London, Connecticut, at a Vassar prom, the year before her graduation. They'd dated as frequently as time and distance would allow, and the summer after Helen's graduation they were married. Some of her more snobbish classmates thought Helen had married beneath her—George's family owned and operated a chain of dry-cleaning establishments—but by and large the difference in their respective statuses hadn't been enough to cause much comment.

They had no children. Recently, Helen's younger sister, Patricia, had come to live with them while she attended a private school in Washington. Patricia was fifteen years old.

The Quentins were popular with the other young marrieds among their neighbors and well thought of by the older people. Helen's work with the League of Women Voters had gained her respect with the less flighty element in the area. Both she and George enjoyed a reputation for being sensible young folks who never threw wild parties or disturbed the proprieties in any other way. There was no hint in Putnam's report that anyone who knew them might be aware of their underground sex activities.

It wasn't much, but by the time Hortense arrived I'd stored it away in the back of my mind anyway. She looked rested and spruced up, but she'd put on the same dress she'd been wearing in the afternoon. Also, she was carrying a model's hatbox-style case, which she put down on the floor just inside the door as she greeted me.

"I don't know how you did it, Steve," she said, "but I guess I'm all yours. The powers that be called and said they were giving me an indefinite leave of absence with the understanding that they'd put me back on the job whenever I was ready."

"And the financial details are all arranged, too," I told her, "so you don't have to worry on that score."

"Great." She shot me a winning smile. "Oh, say," she added, "how about this dress?" She pirouetted slowly, and I'm afraid I studied her impressive figure more than the dress itself. "I put it back on because I wasn't sure just how formal or how sexy you wanted me to be. But I have a cocktail gown in there." She indicated the carrying case. "I can change in a minute, if you want me to."

"You're fine just the way you are," I told her. "Not too flashy, but stylish and appealing."

"Why, thank you, kind sir."

"You can leave the bag here and pick it up later," I told her. "We'd better get going now."

We grabbed a cab downstairs, and on the way out to the upper-crust Chevy Chase neighborhood where the Quentins rented their house I went over our cover-story with Hortense. I'd decided to keep it simple, and Hortense had no trouble getting the details down. In essence, it was as follows:

We'd been married for two years and came from Bloomington, Indiana. I'd picked Indiana because it might open the door to conversation about other Hoosiers known to the members of George and Helen's group. There might even be a lead-in to the missing Cromwells. And I'd decided on Bloomington, rather than the Cromwell's home town of Danville, because it would tie in with my work.

Indiana University, which has a connection with the Kinsey Institute, is in Bloomington. I intended to be honest about my work with O. R. G. Y. if the subject came up, and instructed Hortense to be the same. It would explain my curiosity about a lot of things. And my experience has been that once people relax with the fact that they're being observed, they're kind of flattered by it and cooperate easily. As far as Hortense was concerned, research was my only motive. I didn't see any need to tell her about the other aspects of what I was doing. But I did tell her that I was particularly anxious to arrange entree into another group which might be hipped on "discipline." She, as well as I, was to drop hints that we'd been involved in "discipline clubs" back in Bloomington and were anxious to make a similar connection in Washington. To lend credence to our story, we were to say that I was in Washington in connection with a survey of "punishment" groups which would encompass major cities across the country.

By the time we'd gone over the story two or three times and had everything down pat, the cab pulled up in front of the Quentin house. It was an expensive Spanish colonial abode, and I judged it to be in the $40,000 to $45,000 price range. The grounds covered a half acre, and had been carefully but not ostentatiously landscaped. The house itself was hidden from the street by high hedges and was reached by a circular driveway.

The front door opened as the cab, having discharged us, pulled back down the driveway. A young woman, petite and blonde and with something of an intellectual air about her, stood in the doorway and smiled tentatively at Hortense and myself. "Are you Steve?" she asked as we mounted the three wide steps to the porch.

"Yes," I replied. "And this is my wife, Hortense. I hope you're expecting us. Mr. Vel—"

"You're expected," she said quickly. "Our mutual friend called. I'm Helen." She held out her hand.

I took it and passed it along to Hortense. "I'm happy to meet you, Helen," Hortense said with just the right mixture of warmth and formality.

"We're just a small group tonight," Helen said as she led the way inside. "Only two other couples, but we're all ardent Francophiles. Ah!" she broke off. "Here's George. Come and say hello to Steve and Hortense, George."

A clean-cut Ivy League type entered the large center hallway from the living room. He might have stepped out of a Brooks Brothers window display. His gray suit was conservative, but stylish, and he had the naturally narrow-shouldered sort of build suited to it. He was a little under average height, and his face was boyish, the eyes very alert behind horn-rimmed glasses. I'd have bet it wasn't more than a year or two since he'd given up crew haircuts. Even now his straight brown hair was trimmed very close to his skull.

As we exchanged handshakes and introductions, two things told me right away that Hortense was an excellent choice for this venture. First there was the way George's eyes travelled approvingly over the figure in the green knit dress and stayed lingeringly on the exact spot where the vague outline of her legs joined. Second was the fact that in her high heels Hortense was a couple of inches taller than George. It may be a generalization, but I've rarely met a short man who wasn't attracted to tall girls. At first impression, George was surely no exception.

He and Helen ushered us into the living room and introduced the other guests. Only first names were used. The first couple was identified as Barry and Elsa. Barry was fortyish, a big man, jowly and running to fat. Elsa was in her thirties, on the skinny side, nervous in a bird-like way and given to high-pitched giggles that made her seem even more like a bird because of her habit of shaking her head from side to side so that her close-cropped and curly black hair bristled like a coxcomb as she giggled.

The other couple was Phil and Ingrid. They looked to be the youngest of any of us. Phil had a wet-behind-the-ears air of nervousness about him, the sort of doubtful attitude a teen-age boy might have when approaching his first visit to a brothel. Later I would learn that Phil was far from a novice; that what I had mistaken for apprehension was really high-strung eagerness. His wife, Ingrid, was much calmer. Like him, she seemed very young, but there was a sort of sureness about her. It was this sureness I suppose that kept her from appearing blatantly sexual as compared to the other women. Where they were quietly dressed, Ingrid wore a very low-cut cocktail gown, bright red, which seemed bent on ejecting her grapefruit-sized—and shaped—breasts. Also, her hair, a much brighter blonde than Helen's, was very long and worn loosely so that its strands curled over her voluptuous bosom and accented it. But, as I said, her calm manner kept her from seeming out-and-out brazen.

As Hortense and I sat down and joined the group, George asked if we'd like some martinis. I said yes; Hortense turned him down. As he started for the bar, Elsa held up her glass and giggled that she'd like another.

"Perhaps later, Elsa," he told her. "But not right now. We don't want to spoil things."

"George is really a moralist," Helen explained, sitting down next to me on the small couch. "He doesn't hold with people drinking too much."

"I am not a moralist," George called from the bar. "I just believe in being practical. A minimal amount of liquor relaxes the inhibitions. Past that point, it's self-defeating in terms of sexual potential. Any real swinger knows that."

"In any case, George knows Elsa," Barry boomed out heartily. "Another martini and she'd be all laughs and no action."

"I'm afraid I do tend to get tiddly," Elsa chirped.

"Just enough liquor to whet the appetite without dulling the taste buds," Ingrid said calmly. "That's George's theory. It might seem inhospitable," she said directly to me, "but actually it's one of the things that makes George an excellent party host."

"Ingrid's right about that," Helen told me. "When George would turn somebody down for a drink, it used to embarrass me. But now I realize he's right not to let over-imbibing spoil things. After all, we're not here to get drunk."

"Which brings us to why we are here," Phil said. "Just

what have you and George got planned for the evening? I was telling Ingrid on the way over that I always love it when you host a party because you two can be depended upon to come up with something unusual."

"Well, first," Helen said as George crossed over to me, "I have a new batch of photos from a group I correspond with in Boise, Idaho. I thought we might pair off to look at them. The subjects are from a new French club, and they're refreshingly uninhibited. And the quality of the photos, I think you'll agree, is excellent."

"You mean you want us to go off by couples to look at them?" Phil asked eagerly.

"No. You're always in too much of a hurry, Phil. I simply meant we'd pair off here and pass them around. I'll stay with Steve here. Barry can sit next to Hortense. Phil and Elsa and George and Ingrid can form twosomes."

Everybody shifted around, and then Helen produced a packet of about forty four-by-five photos, all of which were in color. She handed them out, kept some for herself, and then sat back down alongside of me. Our thighs brushed as she leaned close to show me the first picture.

It was quite a picture. It featured a lovely young brunette with her skirt pulled up over her hips. She was wearing no underwear, and a man knelt in front of her. The man's lips were pursed and very close to the clean-shaven area just below her smooth belly. One of the girl's hands was tangled in his hair, and there was a rapturous look on her face.

Helen stroked my thigh quickly, and then went on to the next picture. It was the same couple, only with the situation reversed. Now the man was naked from the waist down and the girl knelt in front of him. His excitation was immense, and her cheeks were stretched wide to encompass it.

In the next picture, both man and girl were completely nude. The girl was crouched over him, her large breasts grazing his shins, her lips fastened to him securely. His head was raised slightly in an effort to return the favor.

"How do you like that, Steve?" Helen asked, her lips hot and moist against my ear.

"Delightful," I told her.

"Later," she promised, "I'll show you some things that are even more delightful."

The same girl was in the next picture, but the man had been replaced by a second girl, a blonde. The original brunette had her mouth pressed to one of the blonde's breasts. The nipple of the other breast stood out a good three-quarters of an inch, and the roseate framing it had turned a flaming red which covered a wide area.

The pictures continued. The two girls performed various acts, then the two men. Then, breathing heavily, Helen exchanged photos with George. The second set of pictures involved yet another couple. The original couple had gotten together with them for these photos and the results were complicated, but well-patterned and practical.

The next two batches of pictures were extreme close-ups involving all six people. As with the other photos, the emphasis remained on oral acts. And there seemed no part of the body which these people had deemed inedible.

"They would like us to send some photos in exchange," Helen announced when we'd finished looking at the pictures. "I thought we might take some at our next meeting, but not tonight. George and I have other things planned for tonight."

"I should hope so," Phil said. "Somehow, I'm always the one who gets stuck taking the pictures."

"Well, you are a photographer," his wife Ingrid reminded him.

"A *baby* photographer," he protested. "And while this sort of thing might not be exactly a busman's holiday, I'd rather participate in the activities than record them."

"All right, smarty, since you're so anxious, you can be the first one to try this new game I've devised," Helen told Phil. "If you win, you can have your pick of any mouth in the room."

"Okay," Phil said. "I'm game. How do I play?"

"George will blindfold you and tie your hands behind your back," Helen told him. "Then each of the women in turn will offer a breast to your mouth only. The length of time it remains will be strictly up to the individual girl. Your object is to identify each of the four of us after it's all over. If you get us right in one-two-three-four order, then you win."

"Do I have to tell right from left?" Phil asked.

"That won't be necessary," Helen laughed.

George blindfolded Phil and tied his hands behind his back. Then he led him over to a chair and seated him across the room from the rest of us. Silently, Helen indicated to the other three women the order in which they were to approach him.

Elsa was first. She unbuttoned her dress and pushed down one side of her bra. The breast she revealed was small but high-slung and with a full, sweeping curve to it. The nipple was a mahogany-brown color, the roseate a delicate tan.

She approached Phil from the side, put her hand under the breast and pushed it in his mouth. Phil's cheeks seemed to pulsate and his lips worked eagerly. Elsa rocked back and forth as she stood in front of him, bending slightly so that as much of her breast as possible would be encompassed. Finally, she clutched her knees together, released a high-pitched giggle and then pulled away.

"Well, that one was easy," Phil said.

Helen shook her head disapprovingly at Elsa as she re-

39

arranged her bra and sat back down. Then she approached Phil herself, as if to show the way it should be done. Her dress had a zipper down the back, and Helen pulled it as she walked across the room. The petite blonde let the top fall to her hips. She wore a slip, but no bra under it. She shrugged one of the slip straps from her shoulder and pushed the breast-flesh out to the side. The breast itself wasn't much larger than Elsa's had been, but it was shaped differently. It was rounder, and the tip was very long. There was no visible roseate, but the tip was scarlet.

It quivered just before she presented it to Phil's lips. Helen only let him sample the tip. When he moved forward to try for more, she moved away and prevented him from getting it. Also, she purposely brushed his cheek with the side of the breast. I realized that by pushing the flesh out that way, Helen was trying to make Phil mistake it for someone else's. Undoubtedly, to a blindfolded man, it would seem much larger than it was.

Helen didn't even try to duplicate the thrill Elsa had gotten. She stood there for about two minutes, very businesslike, and then backed away. Phil looked puzzled after she left.

Ingrid was next. She didn't have to push down the top of her red dress very far to expose both breasts. They were large and round, with a deep cleavage between them. The roseates were also large, pink, and indistinguishable from the nipples, which weren't extended.

As she approached her husband, Helen signaled to her to toss her hair behind her back so that he wouldn't be able to identify her that way. Ingrid followed the suggestion and then offered one breast to Phil's lips. As soon as he had it, she pulled it away. She repeated the maneuver again and again, rhythmically. Watching, I noticed that the tips widened and grew darker in color, but still the nipples didn't distend.

"I know my wife," Phil said positively when Ingrid pulled away for good.

Hortense was last—but definitely not least. She was even larger than Ingrid. Her nipples were bright red and straining even before she reached Phil. They tapered perfectly from roseates that were only a shade less bright. Following Helen's example, she allowed his lips to fasten only on the breast-tip itself. I don't know whether she was putting them on or not, but her hips moved rhythmically all the time she stood there, and she actually did a little bump-and-grind before she moved away.

"Well, Phil?" Helen asked then.

"Elsa was first. I'm sure of that. And my wife was third. But I have to admit I'm guessing with the other two." He paused and then made his guess. "Hortense was second, Helen last," he said.

"Wrong!" George laughed. "It was the other way around. Helen fooled you. You lose." He walked over to Phil and untied his hands.

"Damn!" Phil said as he took off the blindfold. "When the hell did you get so big?" he asked Helen accusingly.

"Let's watch the profanity," Helen said primly. "I don't like it. Now be a good loser, Phil. Even if you didn't win, you're going to enjoy the next phase of this game." She turned to the rest of us. "We girls are going to draw lots to see who goes first," she said. "You men help George get things ready."

George brought out a sheet. We helped him string it so that it divided the room in two. There were four holes about the size of a man's fist cut in it.

"Take off your pants and shorts," George told us when we had the sheet up. "Then stand so that only the necessary parts protrude through the hole in the sheet."

"Who's the lucky girl?" Barry wanted to know.

"We won't know that until later," George told us. "It's part of the game."

41

I took the number three position. Barry was first, going from left to right, George second, and Phil fourth. The three of us angled our heads to watch Barry as the game started.

About all there was to watch was his rather large stomach bumping against the sheet. He gave one particularly violent thrust, and then groaned with disappointment as he was released. George, who was next, didn't move at all. I guess he was keeping all his muscles clenched so as not to react prematurely. I saw him wince, as if he'd been bitten, and then he too stood back from the sheet.

Now it was my turn. The most delicate flick of a tongue-tip caressed me. It darted about knowingly, switching sides, and then staying in the center and growing bolder. I was reacting now, and the tongue ran the length of my passion. Then it retreated and was replaced by knowing lips. First they too were delicate, then bolder and finally I was completely engulfed by them. I strained under the caress, about to explode, and was immediately released. Like Barry, I groaned as my unfulfilled lust slowly subsided.

Phil was last. The first game had over-excited him. When the lips touched him, he immediately clutched at the sheet and released his passion. There was a giggle from the other side of the sheet, as if to say that whichever girl was involved had no doubt about who had such lack of control.

Phil was actually blushing as we rejoined the girls. They teased him for a minute or so, but then Helen interrupted. "The girl we picked identifies the men as follows," she said, reading from a piece of paper. "Barry first, George second, Steve third, and our own over-eager Phil last."

"That's right," Barry told her. "Now, which one of you girls was it?"

"That's for you to guess," Helen told him. "You can

42

draw lots for the order in which you guess. If you guess right, you and the girl who won can go off alone together for a bit—providing, of course, that it doesn't happen to be your wife. If it is, she gets to choose someone else, and so do you."

I was third when the lots were drawn. Phil was first, Barry second, George last. We three men stood to one side while Phil told the girls his guess.

"Wrong," Helen announced. "Next."

Barry guessed and he was also wrong. Then it was my turn. "Helen," I said positively.

"That's right." She called the rest of the men over. "Steve guessed it right," she told them. "And he sounded awfully sure of himself. Were you?" she asked me.

"Yes. I was positive."

"Really? But how could you be?"

"Well, you're the shortest girl here."

"Yes," Helen admitted. "But I was on my knees."

"I allowed for that. Even on your knees, you'd be shorter than any of the other girls if they'd been on their knees."

"But how did that give me away?"

"There was a definite downward pull," I told her. "I noticed it from the way Barry and then George was standing. And I confirmed it for myself when you reached me."

"A Sherlock Holmes!" Helen clapped her hands.

"Elementary, eh what son?" Barry punned.

"Well come on along with me, Sherlock." Helen took my hand. "I'm going to introduce some evidence you'll never forget."

I put on my pants, tucked in my shirt, and followed Helen. She led me back through the central hall and down a corridor with some doors leading off it. There was the sound of a TV set from behind one of the doors, and Helen paused in front of it, frowning. There was a female giggle, and that evidently decided her. "Will you wait just a minute," she said, "while I settle this?"

"Sure."

She pushed the door open, and I had a clear view into the room as she entered. There was a very pretty teenage girl who resembled Helen sitting on the couch. Sitting with her was a boy of roughly the same age. The TV set was on in front of them, but I don't think they were paying too much attention to it. As Helen entered, they were kissing, and the boy's elbow was sticking high up in the air while his hand groped inside the peasant blouse the girl was wearing.

"Patricia!" Helen snapped the name out like a drill sergeant barking a command. "Just what do you think you're doing?"

"Gee, Sis, we didn't hear—" The words tumbled out of the girl's mouth as she tried to re-arrange her clothing. It wasn't easy, because the boy's hand was stuck and he was having trouble getting it out from under the tight bra she wore.

"Of course you didn't hear. This is disgraceful! Leonard, you go home immediately. Patricia, you go up to bed. I'll talk to you in the morning. To think that a sister of mine could behave—" Helen broke off the sentence. "I'll have a lot to say to you tomorrow!" She turned on her heel and rejoined me in the hall.

"These kids today!" she said as she led me into another room. "They have absolutely no morals!" Helen's fingers worked nimbly at my belt until she'd pulled down my pants. "Nothing's sacred to them!" She knelt in front of me and her cheek brushed my naked thigh. "When I was an adolescent girl, virtue meant something!" Her mouth moved over me. "But not any more!" Her lips puckered. "Today girls think no more of losing their virginity than of snapping their fingers!" She snapped her fingers, then made a loose fist out of them and encir-

44

cled me. "There's no controlling them!" Her tongue stayed out on the last word. "Ah-jud dogo wha thigid thi ideez vrub!"

"I beg your pardon?"

"I said I just don't know where they get their ideas from!"

"Neither do I," I agreed as she lowered her head again. "I just don't know what's happening to the youth of to-day. They're so wild."

"Wibd!" Her head bobbed slightly in concurrence.

"Wild!" I repeated. "Wild! Wild! Wild! WILD-wild-WILD-wild-WILD-wild! WI-I-I-I-LD!"

chapter
FOUR

"Do you brush after every meal?" I asked.

It was ten or fifteen minutes later. The door to the connecting bathroom was ajar. Resting idly on the couch, I could see Helen at the sink.

"Yes, I do," she told me as she neatly put the cap back on the toothpaste and replaced it in the medicine cabinet. She rinsed off her toothbrush and put that back, too. "I got in the habit when I was in college. They ran this test, and my half of the class had forty-two percent fewer cavities than the other half, which used Brand X."

"The new scientific ingredient, hey?" I laughed.

"And only Steve has it." She chuckled back. "My favorite dentifrice."

"I'm flattered. But shouldn't we be getting back to the others?" I asked as she came back in and sat down on the couch beside me.

"There's no hurry. Let's have a cigarette first."

That suited me. I gave Helen a light, lit up myself, and then tip-talked up to my real reason for being there. "Do you and George have many couples visiting from out of town like Hortense and me?"

46

"Not too often. It's nice when it happens, though. I like new people. And so does George."

"Ever have anybody from my neck of the woods before?"

"Why do you ask?" Helen looked at me shrewdly.

"Just wondered if we had any acquaintances in common." I kept my voice casual.

"You mean from Indiana? That's where our mutual friend said you were from. What's the scene out there?"

"There are some swingers. But it's mostly calm. Too calm. You know how it is. Everybody's underground. That's why I wondered if you'd met any Hoosiers. I figured I might look them up when I got back home."

"Not really. There was a girl from out that way that Barry brought along one night, but I never got to know her well. She only came the one time, and I don't even remember her name."

"Barry brought a girl? I thought it was strictly married couples?"

"It is. But Elsa was out of town and Barry didn't want to miss out on anything. Tell the truth, I think he called our mutual friend and had him fix it up. George decided the girl wasn't our type, though, and he told Barry not to bring her back again."

"Why wasn't she your type?"

"Too German."

That was all Helen had to say on the subject. It wasn't much to go on, but it might be a lead. Then again, it might not. As I followed Helen back to rejoin the others, I decided I'd just have to go on playing it by ear.

George had organized another variation of Blind Man's Buff, and it was in full swing when Helen and I returned. We sat down on the couch to watch. Across from us, on the other couch, were Ingrid, Elsa and Hortense. They were seated with their dresses pushed up over their hips. None of the three was wearing panties.

Phil, blindfolded, was on his knees in front of them. George was guiding Phil's head to sip at each of them in turn. Then Phil sat back on his heels, thought a moment, and finally spoke.

"Ingrid first, Hortense second, Elsa third," he said.

"Pretty good," Barry chuckled from the sidelines.

"You got it right," George told Phil as he removed the blindfold.

"I'm an expert wine-taster," Phil said smugly. "And the vintage I choose is Hortense."

He led Hortense off to another part of the house. Helen took her place on the couch and beckoned to Barry. The other two girls joined me, and George followed them. "Flip a coin, Elsa," he instructed. "Ingrid, you call it."

"Heads," Ingrid called.

"You win," George told her. As she slipped out of her clothes and lay down on the rug, he turned to me. "Do you prefer left or right?" he asked politely.

"It makes no difference."

"Very well. Then I'll take the left one."

George knelt and took Ingrid's left breast between his lips. I followed his example with the large, quivering right globe. Elsa dined at another part of the shapely table.

Ingrid seemed insatiable. Sighs and moans were followed by a series of cries that shook her whole body again and again. Her breast-tip was rigid, the flesh so hot it seemed to sear my lips. Finally she scrambled to her feet, grabbed me by the hand, and tugged me off to a corner of the room. Here the voluptuous blonde virtually toppled me and slammed down on top of me like a tigress gone berserk. Time dissolved into a mad race we galloped through together. And then it was over and we huddled together, exhausted, in a corner on the rug.

"Look."

I followed Ingrid's pointing finger to where George

and Elsa were running a different sort of race. George had Elsa by the ankles and she was sort of walking on her hands. Each time he lunged, she'd jump another step with her hands. Yet, at the same time, her small, plump *derriere* seemed to move in the other direction, back against him.

"They're too much." Ingrid giggled.

"Is George always so athletic?" I asked.

"New people inspire him."

"But surely Elsa isn't new to him."

"No. But your wife is. I think he's just working himself up to take care of Hortense."

"Have you ever seen him with a new girl?"

"Yes. Once. There was this girl Barry brought. But George was disappointed in her, though."

"She swung the wrong way?" I made it sound like a guess.

"That's right. She was one of those punishment nuts."

"Yeah. Helen mentioned her," I admitted. "Said she came from Indiana. You don't happen to remember her name, do you?"

"Don't tell me you dig that sort of thing?" Ingrid drew away from me a little.

"No. I'm just wondering if I know this chick. After all, she is a fellow Hoosier."

"Oh. Well, her name was Carrie."

Carrie! Now it really felt like I might be getting warm. Carrie was Cromwell's wife's name. "Sort of a goody-goody type with mouse-brown hair?" I asked Ingrid.

"She had brown hair, all right. But there was nothing prissy about this girl. She was too far out for our clique."

"She didn't happen to mention her last name, did she?"

"Don't be silly." Ingrid looked at me suspiciously. "How come you ask so many questions?" she wanted to know.

49

"It's his business to ask questions." Phil had returned with Hortense, and he'd answered Ingrid before I could. "He's a sex investigator from an outfit called O. R. G. Y."

"What?" It was a general echo that ran around the room as everybody stopped what they were doing and more or less broke apart to turn their attention to me.

"You said it would be all right to tell them, Steve," Hortense said. "I hope I didn't goof."

"You didn't," I assured her. "But I guess I'd better explain to these good people—"

"What kind of sex investigator? . . . He's some kind of spy! . . . What's this O. R. G. Y.? . . . They're undercover agents! . . . Why did they have to pick on us? . . . A government check of some kind! . . . What are they after? . . . Like that security shake-up with the queers in the State Department! . . ."

The questions and the accusations flew thick and fast. It was a few minutes before I could get them calmed down enough to listen to me. When they finally did, it still took quite a while before I could convince them that we weren't out to blackmail them, or prosecute them, or make public their activities, or hurt them in any way. "We're just compiling data," I assured them over and over again. "We don't want to curtail your activities. If anything, this survey by O. R. G. Y. should result in a wider tolerance of private sex practices by groups such as yours."

Finally they relaxed with it. George Putman, who was a lawyer, pointed out to the others that Hortense and I had been willing accessories to the evening's activities and therefore couldn't harm them legally without implicating ourselves. With this assurance the general attitude changed from suspicion to a willingness to cooperate, a willingness born of their being flattered by our "professional" interest in their activities. Indeed, during the next phase of the fun and games, they outdid themselves in trying to impress us.

This was particularly noticeable with Elsa. The bird-like little woman insisted on devoting herself to "entertaining" both Hortense and myself at the same time. The others rested, chatted, watched, and made good-natured remarks as Elsa introduced us to "a few innovations for the benefit of your study."

She took a jar of honey, coated her inner thighs and palpitating womanhood with it, and then applied it liberally to the matching area of my body. She then curled up beside me and sipped the honey. At the same time, she had Hortense sample her own sweetness. It's hard to explain in words, but there was definitely something about the stickiness that was more than ordinarily arousing. I could tell that even Hortense was carried away by it. Certainly Elsa was omniverous. And as for myself, despite my depleted resources, Elsa's appetite was so uninhibitedly expressed that I couldn't help being inspired to satisfy it.

When it was over, the petite "swinger" bounced up beside me on the couch and whispered in my ear. "They're a little square around here," she murmured. "If you really want something wild for your survey, I could arrange for you two to meet some real strong people."

That was what I'd been hoping for. The key word was "strong." Who'd ever have thought that Elsa might provide entry to the discipline underground?

"Will it be all right with Barry?" I whispered back.

"Why not? He likes your wife. I can tell."

"And you're not jealous?"

"Are you kidding? I make an occasional scene without Barry. And the other way around, too. We don't bug each other."

51

"This group you're talking about—is Carrie a member of it?"

"How did you know about Carrie?"

"She's a fellow Hoosier." I said it as if it explained everything. "Will she be there?"

"I don't know. She's no particular friend of mine. Barry likes her."

Just about then they began re-shuffling partners again. I took advantage of their preoccupation and stole a couple of minutes' whispered conversation with Hortense. "Try to pair off with Barry," I told her. "See if you can get anything out of him about a Hoosier girl who digs spanking and such. Her name's Carrie."

"Steve, just what are you getting me into?" Hortense looked at me quizzically.

"This is no time for explanations," I pointed out.

"Okay." She shrugged. "I'll see what I can find out."

Claiming visitor's privileges, Hortense grabbed off Barry for the next round. I took a back seat with George and Phil while the three ladies staged an exhibition for us. It was quite a show—sort of a gourmet's delight of female sexuality.

After that, the party broke up. George called a cab for us, and when Hortense and I were alone in the back of it, I asked her what she'd learned from Barry.

"Not much," she told me. "He knows a girl from Indiana named Carrie. Says she's married and digs discipline, but her husband doesn't. They don't like having her around for that reason. The other wives object to an extra female. He says he hasn't seen her for a while and doesn't know if she'll be at the next meeting of the discipline society. We're invited, incidentally. He gave me this phone number so you can call him tomorrow and get the details. He said his wife mentioned it to you."

"She did." I took the number. "I'll call him, and then

I'll give you a ring. What did you think of the evening?" I added idly.

"I've never been so shocked in my life," Hortense said primly.

"You've got to be kidding. After all, you're a professional."

"That's right. And in all my professional life I've never met such depraved, immoral, unethical people! After all, they are married!"

"Hortense, you slay me!" I kissed her impulsively. "It isn't anything they did that bugs you. Right? It's the fact that they're married."

"I suppose so. After all, marriage should be sacred."

"Are you trying to tell me you've never had married men among your clientele?"

"Of course I have. But they didn't bring their wives along to watch them perform."

"Hortense!" I had just made a great discovery. "You're a prude!"

"I just have certain very high standards in some areas. Is there anything wrong with that?"

"Not a thing, sweetie. Not a blessed thing. It just completes the circle, that's all."

"Circle? What circle?"

"The morality circle. You see, for a long time psychologists and sociologists have known that bluenoses are so anti-sex because they're basically lechers at heart. 'Way down deep they want the very vice they attack, only they're too filled with self-doubt to indulge in it. Now you're showing me the other side of the coin. By most standards, you're a pretty free-wheeling chick, not to say downright promiscuous, albeit in a business sense. But underneath, you're really a double-barreled moralist. It reminds me of something I discovered when I was in jail once."

"You were in jail? What for?"

"Speeding, believe it or not. They gave me three days, as an object lesson. And they stuck me in one of those detention homes where they keep all kinds of criminals awaiting trial. Yeah, there were all types there. Murderers and bank robbers and junkies and strongarm men and kids who'd stolen cars and rapists and wife-beaters —all kinds. But every one of them had one thing in common. They each had their own particular screwed-up moral code."

"What do you mean?"

"The bank robber could see how a man might steal, but he was intolerant of any other kind of crime. Rape was downright sinful, and as for murder—well, the most ardent proponent of capital punishment I ever met was a bank robber I got to talking to in the exercise yard. My cell-mate, on the other hand, had knocked off his boss and two cops who tried to stop him. He could understand murder perfectly—it was always a crime of passion, always the result of temporary insanity, he said— but wife-beating? All he asked was the chance to be left alone with one of those wife-beaters; he'd knock their teeth down their throats, the cowardly bullies! The junky thought other crimes disgusting and didn't consider himself a criminal at all; the embezzler thought the junky should be locked up for life with the key thrown away; and the second-story man thought the embezzler was chicken and should be made to pay additionally for his cowardice and underhandedness. . . . Well, I guess you get the idea. You see what I mean?"

"Yes." Hortense frowned. "But what's it got to do with me?"

"Just this. You rationalize what you do in sex, but condemn others for what they do. And, of course, they do the same to you."

"Well, maybe you're right. But there's something else, too."

"What?"

"I'm a professional and these people are amateurs. I don't like them horning in on my business."

"At least you're honest." I laughed. "I'll call you tomorrow after I talk to Barry," I added as the cab pulled up in front of her hotel.

"I'll be waiting." She blew me a kiss and ran up the stairs to the lobby.

I told the driver to take me on to the Windsor. When he dropped me, I went straight up to my room and to bed. I was pooped, and I fell asleep immediately.

The telephone woke me. It was just beginning to get light outside. I answered it with a sleepy grunt.

"Victor?" It was Putnam's voice.

"Yeah."

"Identify yourself."

"Huh?"

"The code word."

"Code word?"

"Is this Steve Victor?"

"Look, Putnam, don't play games. What do you want?"

"The password. I want to be sure I'm talking to you."

"Oh, hell!" I remembered then. "American original. Now, what is it?"

"Victor, if there's one thing I can't abide, it's sloppiness. And you have been unforgiveably sloppy."

"You remind me of my mother," I yawned. "My mother was a lot like you. Now, what the blue blazes are you talking about?"

"Murder, that's what! I don't mind a little killing when it's necessary, Mr. Victor. But in our line of work, you should remember that discretion is the better part of murder. If one must kill, then one does so quietly, and with finesse. One doesn't make a carnival out of it."

"I'll keep it in mind." I yawned again. "Now, if that's all, can I go back to sleep?"

"Certainly not. And you're taking this altogether too lightly, Mr. Victor. Believe me, the police will not be sympathetic to your attitude. It's going to be very difficult to persuade them not to lock you up and throw away the key. They don't like having prominent citizens slain —not even by agents in the service of the government."

"Are you trying to tell me that I bumped off somebody?"

"Yes. And evidently every bit as crudely as you've just phrased it. A sloppy bit of work, Mr.—"

"Now wait a minute! I didn't kill anybody. Not lately, anyway."

"You didn't kill George Quentin last night?"

"Kill Quen—. Of course not. The last I saw of him he was alive and kicking up his heels. Now, suppose you tell me what this is all about."

There was a long pause. Then— "Get dressed and meet me out at Quentin's place right away."

The receiver clicked in my ear. I stared at it for a minute, and then started moving. Less than an hour later a cab was dropping me off back at the Quentin home.

The place was lousy with cops. Putnam was there already, too, which was lucky for me. It was lucky because, if he hadn't been there, as soon as the cops found out who I was they probably would have come down on me like the proverbial ton of bricks. And they found out right away, thanks to two female finger-pointers.

The first was Patricia, Helen Quentin's fifteen-year-old sister. She took one look at me, her finger shot out, and her voice went screeching up the scale as if she'd just spied a stray Beatle strumming into view. "That's him!" she screamed hysterically. "That's the man! That's the man who killed George!"

56

Before I had a chance to tell her that being an adolescent was no excuse for acting like an adolescent, her big sister was coming in on the refrain. She was calmer, but just as positive. "That's Steve Victor, all right," she told a cop-ish looking type. "That's the man who killed my husband." Even as she said it, her eyes were reminiscing over my body.

"Let's go in here where we can talk." Putnam ushered the boss Sherlock and me into an empty room.

"Okay, let's have it," I said when he'd closed the door behind us.

Putnam nodded at the homicide cop and sat back to listen. The cop pulled out some notes and consulted them from time to time as he spoke. "You left here at twelve-thirty last night with a young lady you claimed was your wife," he began.

"That's right."

"You returned shortly after two a. m. and—"

"That's wrong."

"Just listen, Mr. Victor. Don't interrupt." Putnam's voice was weary.

I listened.

"George Quentin admitted you," the homicide cop continued. "You had words. You threatened him. Loudly enough so that you awakened the other members of the household. Quentin's sister-in-law came downstairs. She claims she saw you holding a gun on Quentin and twisting his nose. She says you seemed to be trying to extract some sort of information from him."

"I was probably just checking his sinuses," I said.

The cop shot me a disapproving look and continued. "The kid ran upstairs and got her sister, Quentin's wife. She came down and entered the room where you were. She greeted you by name and you turned around and slugged her. You knocked her unconscious. The kid was

57

still in the hall, not knowing what to do, and she saw this. Then you gave Quentin a jab in the kidneys with the gun and told him he'd better tell you what you wanted to know, or else. He protested that he didn't know anything. The kid says she heard both of you mention the name Cromwell. But she says Quentin kept protesting he didn't know anybody by that name. Well, you started really pistol-whipping the poor guy. But you must have given him one slash too much, 'cause all of a sudden he doubled over and blood began pouring out of his mouth. The kid screamed. That scared you and you bolted out of there. Quentin died. The coroner says he thinks you ruptured his spleen."

"I'd never do a thing like that to dear old George," I said.

"How well did you know him?" the cop asked.

"Not well. I just met him. He was a superb host. That's about all I know about him."

"Okay. Be a wise guy," the cop said. "It doesn't matter. We got you dead to rights. Two witnesses—and one actually saw you kill him."

"Putnam," I said plaintively, "I'm in trouble."

"That you are!" the cop confirmed.

"As usual," Putnam sighed. "Well, you'll just have to go through the formalities," he told me. "There can't be any official cognizance taken of your position."

"What formalities?" I squeaked. "Like getting hung for a murder I didn't commit, maybe?"

"You were seen committing it," the cop reminded me.

"Putnam, will you please tell him—"

"No!" Putnam's voice was quick and firm. "And neither will you! Don't even mention it. Just go along with him and don't worry."

So that's what I did. I went through the formalities. And I didn't tell the cops about my Russian double. I

58

played it that way because that's the way that Putnam wanted it. All the same, I was getting pretty nervous by the time Putnam finally pulled enough strings to get the cops to let me go. I'd shot the whole day playing cat-and-mouse with cops who'd just been itching to give me the third degree. The only thing that had stopped them was their conceit at being criminologists, rather than strong-arm men. But their conceit was wearing pretty thin by the time Putnam finally came through.

It was nightfall when they finally let me creep out of the jailhouse. I made a beeline for the nearest telephone and called the number Barry had given Hortense.

But Barry wasn't home, and neither was Elsa. The maid who answered told me they'd gone out somewhere with another couple. No, she didn't know who the other couple was; she'd never seen them before. The girl had dark red hair; that was all she could tell me.

So I got some more change and called my girl with the dark red hair. "Is Hortense there?" I asked the female who answered.

"No. You just missed her. She went out."

"Do you know where she went?"

"No."

"Do you know who she went with?"

"Yes, but I don't think I'll say. Hortense might not like it. Who's calling, anyway?"

"Just tell her Steve Victor."

"Steve Victor? Are you kidding?"

"No. Why?"

"Because that's who she went out with. Steve Victor. They left here together not an hour ago. Is this some kind of a gag or something?"

"Are you sure?"

"Sure I'm sure. Hortense introduced me to him. She ought to know who she's going out with, shouldn't she?"

59

"Yes, she should." I thanked her and hung up. Yes, I told myself, Hortense should certainly know Steve Victor when she saw him. But what she didn't know was that I was twins and that one of me was a Russian killer.

The wrong one!

The one with Hortense!

chapter
FIVE

So I was the odd twin out. Somewhere in the Washington area my diabolical double was following up my lead with the help of a duped Hortense and a spank-happy married couple who thought he was me, the sex-researcher from O. R. G. Y. But where? How could I pick up their trail?

It was a slim chance, but the only one I could think of who might conceivably point an arrow for me was the bookseller, Martin Velvet. I was sure he would know of any underground discipline clubs operating in the D. C. district or its suburbs. Getting him to part with the information might be something else again, but I decided it was worth the old boola-boola try. I hopped a cab over to U and Eleventh Streets.

I didn't exactly expect Velvet to greet me with open arms, but I didn't expect the greeting I did get, either. He was just getting ready to shut down for the night when I came through the door. It was probably early for him to be doing that, but I guess he wasn't feeling too well. My guess stemmed from the fact that he looked as if some ardent gymnast had been using his face for a trampoline. The parts of it that weren't covered with adhesive bandages or iodine were swelling prettily in a multitude of colors. His visage was as rainbowed a collection of boo-boos as I've ever seen. I had no chance to commiserate, though. The minute I came through the door, Velvet picked up a very large gun from under the counter and pointed it quite accurately at my large intestine.

"What do you want now?" His voice was old chalk on a dry blackboard.

"I just wanted to talk to you." I eyed the cannon. "That's kind of a hard sell, isn't it?"

"High pressure." His voice was firmer now. "You think you can come in here and pressure me any time you want? I'm ready for you this time. No sale! Now beat it!"

"That's no way to treat a good customer."

"Customer? Peddler, you mean! And I don't like the merchandise!" Velvet touched one of the lumps on his cheek meaningfully and pushed the cannon forward an inch or so. "I oughta blast you just for this," he said bitterly. "But I can do without the cops coming around and asking questions. So just beat it and don't come back."

"Did I do that?" I asked. "Did I give you a going-over?"

"Are you nuts?" The expression on his face answered his own question affirmatively. "You think you can come in here and work me over and then act like it never happened? I oughta blast you just for kicks. Just the way you fell on me just for kicks."

"What did I want?" I asked.

"You really are a loony! First I sell you a contact. Then you come back here and push me around because you lost the address and you don't want to pay a small fee to get it again. And now you come back like it never happened. You're nuts! Really nuts!"

I gave what he said a quick ponder. It came up snake-eyes—double trouble. My Russky twin had really been earning his rubles. He must have gotten the Quentins' address from Velvet and picked up from there. He'd stolen Velvet's address from me, and now he'd not only caught up with me, but was one step ahead. And Velvet was the only one who might be able to help me catch up to him.

"Now look, Velvet—" I started to say in a conciliatory tone.

"Look nothing!" He clicked the safety off the gun. "Just get the hell out of here! Fast!"

"Can't we just—" I took half a step toward him.

"One more step and I shoot. I mean it."

I didn't believe him. I should have. I took a step. His finger tightened on the trigger.

I threw myself to one side. The bullet whizzed past my hip-bone. In its wake there was a neat little hole in my best sport jacket. I didn't wait for Velvet to fire again. I jumped the counter and made a grab for the gun.

I missed, but I managed to get a hold on the wrist of the hand grasping it. We wrestled. Fear lent Velvet a wiry strength. But then loaded guns make me pretty chicken, too. I matched him grunt for groan as we wrestled for the pistol.

Almost, I succeeded in wrenching it away from him. But he was too fast for me. Just as I out-muscled him, he managed to pull his wrist free and fling the gun away from both of us. It went hurtling out of sight somewhere among the bookshelves.

Its flight relaxed me. That was a mistake, too. Velvet may not have been out for blood with the gun gone, but he was still bent on getting away from me. Now he scrambled free and dived through a door to the rear of the store. I had no choice but to follow.

There was a large, gloomy storeroom lined with bins. The bins were overflowing with books. I couldn't spot

Velvet as I entered. I knew he was still there right away, though. I knew it because a book came flying out of the shadows and conked me square on the noggin.

Momentarily dazed, I picked it up. *Games People Play* by Eric Berne, M. D. "Apropos", I muttered to myself. I ducked my head as a second book followed the trajectory of the first. *Handbook of Non-Violence*, I noticed as it just missed the tip of my nose. "Hypocrite!" A third literary missile followed. *Thus Spake Zarathustra*. Friend Velvet evidently wasn't very consistent in his literary selections.

Retaliation was in order. I grabbed up a copy of Philip Roth's *Letting Go* from one of the bins and let go. Velvet avoided it and fired back *Das Kapital*. I responded with *Atlas Shrugged*. Copies of *Mission to Moscow* and *Mein Kampf* passed each other in mid-air. *Conscience of a Conservative* and *The Affluent Society* didn't pass each other; they collided.

I fired off Sandburg's *Lincoln*, Wright's *Black Boy* and *Manchild in the Promised Land* in quick succession. Velvet responded with *God and Man at Yale* and *Up from Liberalism*. I found myself ducking like crazy to get out of Buckley's way. Then he shot *Your F. B. I. in Peace and War* at me, and I really got mad.

"Take that!" I launched volumes by Sartre, Kierkegaard and Camus in rapid-fire order. His return barrage was the last straw. It started with *The Man from O. R. G. Y.* and went right through the collected works of Ted Mark all the way up to *Dr. Nyet*.

"Fiend!" I yelled. "Sacrilege!" I was beside myself. "What are these doing in the storeroom anyway? Why aren't they displayed in the window?" I didn't wait for an answer. I picked up a thick, bound volume of *The Compleat Works of Shakespeare as Edited by Bowdler* and bounced it solidly off Velvet's cranium. He went down to the floor in a pile of books and stayed there.

I went over to him. He was out like a light. I dragged him to the back of the storeroom. There was a door leading to a small office there. I pulled Velvet through the doorway and deposited him on a rickety couch in the office.

There was a desk there with an old filing cabinet standing beside it. I began opening the drawers of the cabinet. The top three drawers opened easily to reveal various records and bills and correspondence having to do with the bookstore. The bottom drawer was locked.

I went through Velvet's pockets and came up with a key-ring. The third key I tried unlocked the file drawer. I pulled it open. It was filled with folders arranged in alphabetical order. Not knowing where else to begin, I tried "Q" for Quentin.

The entries on the card under that designation were pretty confusing to me. Velvet must have had some way of coding them known only to him. There were dates and first names—usually by couple—and some figures with dollar signs beside them. The last entry on the card had yesterday's date, my first name, and "$150" alongside it. The top of the card, under the names "George and Helen Quentin" had a series of letters which would probably be meaningful only to Velvet himself.

I studied the list of names a second time. Some of them I recognized. "Barry and Elsa" appeared several times, as did "Phil and Ingrid." But then I noticed some variations. There were two notations of "Barry and Carrie" with two different dates. Next to the second week was an asterisk with the abbreviation "ger." beside it. I guessed that it might stand for "German" and have something to do with the discipline club Barry had taken Carrie to visit. And that was probably the same one friend Barry had taken my double and Hortense to tonight.

Farther down the card there was another discrepancy. The names "Ingrid and Phil" appeared together quite a

65

few times, but here was the entry "Ingrid and Knute," with another asterisk followed by "sw." in very small letters.

Knute! It clicked. It was an uncommon name. It was also the name of the Swedish engineer that Putnam had said was the man who'd alerted the Pentagon to the value of Cromwell's invention. Could it be the same man?

Could be, I decided. And if so, there was something very rotten in the state next door to Denmark. I decided to revive friend Velvet and see what light he might shed on this smorgasbord.

I decided too late. While I'd been poring over the Quentin file, Velvet had rustled himself up out of Tweet-Tweet Land and crawled behind the desk. By the time I spotted him, he'd already yanked the lever of a burglar alarm there. The atmosphere of the bookshop was suddenly filled with a loud whooping like seasick cranes sounding out a "May Day."

In the din, Velvet cowered away from me, but the expression on his face was vindictive, to say the least. I wagged a finger at him disapprovingly, spotted a back door leading to an alley, and bounded away from the scene as fast as my $10.95 Thom McCanns could carry me. The cops were sure to come leap-frogging up at any minute, and I'd had enough of cops for one day. The police station may be an interesting place to visit, but I wouldn't want to live there.

When I'd put enough distance between myself and the asthmatic howls of the burglar-alarm banshees, I slowed down and looked for a phone booth. I found one in a drugstore and dialed Putnam. His line was busy. I had a Coke at the counter, and then tried him again. This time he answered.

"American original," I identified myself.

"You grow sloppier, Mr. Victor," he said in a voice that showed the strain of being kept under control.

"That's how it is with bad habits," I told him. "They get worse."

"Don't be flip, Mr. Victor. Your latest escapade really distresses me. First an inept killing, and now a messy assault! I have just gotten off the telephone with the police, and they are most irate."

"Word gets around fast."

"I don't really see why it should be necessary for you to persist in such behavior, Mr. Victor."

"Look, if you'll stop slapping my hand a minute, let me remind you that I didn't kill Quentin. Also, I didn't assault Velvet—at least not the first time."

"But you did attack him tonight," Putnam pointed out.

"Nope. I only defended myself. He threw a few books at me. I threw a few back. My aim was better than his. That's all."

"And you rifled his office. Correct?"

"Correct," I granted. "So give me two demerits. I'm a naughty spy. I never denied it."

"Your conduct really does leave a lot to be desired," Putnam admonished me.

"That's because my upbringing was over-permissive. But what the hell, Mr. Putnam, you wouldn't want to break my spirit, would you?"

"I don't want to spoil you, either. After all, in our line of work, we must be prepared to cope with reality, to deal with society as it really is. You must learn to exercise a little tact in your escapades, Mr. Victor."

"I'll try," I promised. "Now, to get down to the tacky brass, I would like the address of Knute Hajstrom. I wish to have words with the Scandinavian gentleman."

"Oh? Why, Mr. Victor?"

"It would take too long to explain."

"Very well." Putnam gave me the address. "But please be careful how you conduct yourself with Mr. Hajstrom," he cautioned me. "Our relations with the Swedes are very good. I shouldn't like to see them jeopardized."

"Kid gloves up to the elbows," I assured him.

"Hands off altogether, if you don't mind," he said firmly. "You are not to use any kind of force with him."

"Okay," I promised. I hung up then and left the drugstore. I hopped a cab to the address Putnam had given me. It turned out to be a residence hotel. The desk clerk, a laconic type whose jaws were welded together by a huge wad of chewing gum, informed me through his teeth that Hajstrom had gone out.

"Do you know where he went?" I asked.

"Nope."

"Do you know where he went?" I repeated the question and passed a five-dollar bill over the counter.

He tucked the bill neatly into his back pocket. "Nope," he repeated in exactly the same toneless voice.

"Did he go out alone?"

"Nope."

"Who'd he go out with?"

He popped his gum and looked significantly toward the breast pocket in which I'd replaced my wallet. I took out another five, but this time I held onto it. "Who'd he go out with?" I dangled the bill just out of reach.

"A dame. I don't know her name."

"Have you seen her before?"

"She's been here a coupla times."

"Describe her." I moved the five a little closer, but not close enough for him to grab it.

"Young. Blonde. Snazzy. Boobies out to here." He snapped his gum again. "Wears a wedding ring. Shows everything she got, which is plenty."

It could be Ingrid, all right. "Anything else you can tell me?" I asked.

"Nope."

"Okay." I handed him the five. "Buy yourself a stick of chewing gum," I told him.

"Never use it." He popped his gum at my back insultingly as I left.

What now? I strolled idly up the street, mulling over the possibilities. Hortense and the Russian were whipping it up somewhere with Barry and Elsa. They might be on Cromwell's trail—or at least on his wife Carrie's trail—but that didn't help me any; I had no way of catching up with them. Likewise, Hajstrom and Ingrid might be someplace important, but again I'd come up against a dead end. Velvet? He was probably busy lying to the cops. But what about Phil? Ingrid's husband? The only trouble was, I didn't know his last name, or where they lived, either. Another blind alley.

Well, what did I know? I knew Helen Quentin, that's what. And I knew her address. Of course, she thought I'd killed her husband, which might make getting her to cooperate a little difficult. Then again, that might work to my advantage. If she was scared enough of me, she might tell me what I wanted to know just to get rid of me. Well, some of what I wanted to know, anyway—only some, because I sure wanted to know a helluva lot at this point.

There was a snazzy convertible parked in the Quentin driveway when the cab dropped me off. I perked up at the sight of it. I'd noticed it parked there the night before, too. It wasn't the Quentins' car. I could see both of their cars sticking out of the garage. So it had to belong to one of the couples I'd met the night before. That was good, because right now I'd settle to talk to either one of them.

I rang the bell. The door opened. It started to shut again right away. I stuck my foot in fast. Another foot cracked against my shinbone. Cursing, I slammed my shoulder against the door. The motion carried me into the house and smack up against my old playmate, Phil.

"Consoling the widow?" I guessed as I slammed him up against the foyer wall.

"Who is it, Phil?" Helen Quentin's voice coming from the living room didn't sound as bereaved as it might have.

Something hard jabbed against my leg from Phil's pocket. I cracked his wrist hard with a karate chop as he reached for the pocket, and then removed the object myself. It was a nice, shiny, little black revolver.

"Now what kind of thing is this for a baby photographer to be toting around?" I clucked as I backed off and pointed the gun at him. "You want to scare the tots?"

"I—I only brought it along because Helen was nervous." His voice quavered. "That's why I'm here. Because she's afraid."

"Let's see just how afraid she is." I motioned him toward the living room and followed him inside.

"Oh, no!" Helen Quentin shot to her feet as we entered and backed away from me. She seemed genuinely frightened.

Under the circumstances, that might have been perfectly natural. Only there was one detail about the recent widow that wasn't natural at all. She was wearing only a bra and panties, and nothing else!

"Naughty, naughty," I told them. "And poor George hardly cold in his coffin yet."

"George," she murmured more to herself than to me, "was cold long before they put him in his coffin."

"He didn't seem that way last night," I pointed out.

"He was fine in group situations. But person-to-person, he was strictly deep-freeze."

"What do you want?" Phil demanded. He strode over to Helen and put his arm around her protectively.

"Touching," I remarked. "Very touching. And," I added to Helen, "I admire your widow's weeds very much."

"What do you want?" she echoed Phil's question. Her voice was braver now, but she was still frightened.

I came right to the point. "Hortense went to some sort of discipline group with Barry and Elsa tonight. I want to know where they meet."

Helen and Phil both looked blank.

"Barry once brought a girl named Carrie here. He took her to the same place. What do you know about it?"

"Nothing." Helen sounded like she was telling the truth.

"If Barry swings that way, he keeps it quiet." Phil backed her up.

"Honest," Helen said, "he wouldn't tell any of us. George was very strict. He wouldn't have had Barry and Elsa in the house if he thought they were spankers. He didn't dig that."

"Do you?" I asked.

"No."

"What about you, old buddy?" I asked Phil.

"Not my dish."

I thought about whether or not to believe them. I decided I might as well. As far as I knew, they had no reason to lie. But before I could get on to the next question, Helen came up with one of her own.

"How did you get out of jail?" she asked.

"I had Tonto back Silver up to the window and kick the bars in," I told her blithely. "Anything else you want to know?"

"Yes. Why did you kill George?"

"He had post-nasal drip. It was incurable. He didn't want you to know. I did him a favor."

"How can you talk to her that way?" Phil asked indignantly. "Don't you have any sensitivity?"

"I guess I'm just not as broken up over poor old George as you two are," I told him pointedly.

He flushed, and they both fell silent.

"What about your Frau tonight?" I asked Phil.

"What about her?"

"How come she didn't come along with you to help console the widow?"

Now it was his turn to shoot me a who's-kidding-whom look.

"I withdraw the question. But tell me, where is Ingrid?"

"She went out." Phil shrugged. "I don't know where."

"You don't sound like you care much, either."

"We don't get on each other's backs."

"Very sensible. But surely you must have some idea of where she'd be likely to go on her own."

"Why should you be interested in Ingrid?" he wanted to know.

"That's my business. Let's just say I am. Now answer the question." I wiggled the gun to encourage him.

"I'm really not sure."

"Do you know a friend of hers named Knute Hajstrom?" I tried another tack.

"Yeah. I've met him. I don't know him very well, though."

"What's his connection with Ingrid?"

"She's a Svenska—or, at least, her parents were. She met him at some affair thrown by an outfit called Friends of Sweden. She goes there every so often, and I guess she sees him there."

"Don't you go with her?"

"I went a couple of times. I didn't dig it. Now she goes by herself."

Noticing the way he dropped his eyes, I played parlor psychiatrist. "You're not telling me something, Philsy," I tutted at him. "If you hold back, I'm going to get very angry."

"Oh, all right. There's an angle to this Swedish group. Ingrid got involved with them through Velvet's mailing service, the same as we got involved with Helen here and George. Only they swing a different way."

"Like how?" I wanted to know.

"The body beautiful. They dig voyeurism more than anything. They go for stripping and chasing each other around in the buff with polaroids and stuff like that. But the hang-up is there's never any personal contact. I just can't see it."

"But Ingrid can. Right?"

"I guess so. She gets some kind of narcissistic kick out of watching the guys ogle her and get all hot and bothered. I think she gets more of a kick out of that than out of any other kind of sex."

"And that's where she might be tonight, hey?" I ignored his noncommittal shrug. "Well, Philsy-boy, suppose you just give me the address and tell me how I get into the place."

"If I do, will you get out of here and leave us alone?"

"Scout's honor," I assured him.

"How do I know I can trust you?"

"You don't." I wiggled the gun at him. "But you don't have much choice, now do you?"

"I guess not." He sighed. "All right." He rattled off an address. "Just give them this." He took a card out of his wallet and handed it to me.

It was a business card from the Velvet Book Mart. On the back of it were the letters "sw." with "O.K., M.V." scrawled underneath. "The 'sw.' stand for Swedish'?" I asked Phil.

"Yeah." He stuck his chin out. "You going to go away and leave us alone like you said you would now?" he asked.

"I'm on my way," I assured him. "Anything I can tell your wife for you?"

"Yeah. Tell her you never saw me. She can be sticky when it comes to Helen here."

73

"I thought you said she didn't care."

"You've got it backwards," he told me. "She doesn't care about me. It's Helen she gets jealous about."

"Gee, it must be nice to be loved by so many people," I told Helen sincerely.

"And in so many different ways," she giggled.

"Ingrid could have fooled me," I admitted.

"She did fool me," Phil said with a touch of bitterness. "But don't get the wrong idea. She's not a real Les; just a switch-hitter; and pretty particular about it, too. Helen's the only woman I ever saw her really go ape for. Not that I can blame her," he added, giving Helen a little squeeze.

"Well, at least it's all in the family," I said philosophically as I started out the door.

"Hey, what about giving me back my gun," Phil called after me.

"Some other time," I yelled back. "You've got your hands full now."

I slammed the door behind me and started down the driveway. I must have walked for twenty minutes before I finally found a taxi. It was another twenty before it dropped me off at the address Phil had provided.

It was a rundown factory district, deserted and quiet with the lack of activity that came with the night. There was a sign painted on the door of the building the cab dropped me at. It said *Swedish Massage Parlor*. I knocked and the door opened just enough so that a nose-tip could stick out.

"*Ja?*" the nosetip asked.

I slipped the card Phil had given me through the crack. The door opened all the way, and I followed a pair of musclebound shoulders down a long, dingy hallway. Another door was opened, and my guide stood aside to let me through.

It was a large, brightly lit room. There were twenty-odd people of both sexes bouncing around it. About half of them were completely nude. The other half were getting there. A few of the men were running around with cameras. They were very enthusiastic. They were chasing three or four squealing girls, who occasionally paused to pose coyly and then gamboled out of range.

As I was taking it all in, a healthy Nordic type bounced a breast off my elbow and whispered a greeting into my ear. "Why don't you get comfortable?" she suggested.

"I will," I assured her. "But first I'm looking for some friends. Knute and Ingrid. Do you know them?"

"Oh, sure. They're in the trophy room." She pointed.

I crossed over to the archway she'd indicated and paused to read the plaque nailed over it. *Swedish Sport Club*, it said. I pushed through the curtains and went into the trophy room.

It was lit very softly. Also, it seemed very crowded. A small room to start with, it had so many cups and statuettes and antique guns and other junk crammed into it that there hardly seemed room enough to move around.

I noticed a fencing foil hanging on the wall opposite me. The wall was very dusty, and there was the outline of another saber which must have crossed it but had been recently removed. I wondered idly why it had been taken down.

Then I stopped wondering. I saw the missing saber. It was sticking straight up from the chest of a man lying on the couch.

A mackerel couldn't have been any deader than he was.

All the same, I crossed over to make sure. I pulled the blade out of his chest and bent over automatically, but without hope, to listen for a heartbeat. What I heard was a loud scream.

I whirled around, still holding the bloody saber by the hilt. Ingrid was standing just inside the curtain. She screamed again. Then she managed to come up with some words. "It's you!" she said. "First you killed George, and now Knute!" Then she screamed the third time.

"Knute?" I was having a rough time catching up with the rest of the class. "You mean this is Knute Hajstrom?"

She nodded mindlessly. Then she turned her scream into the age-old cry. "Help! Murder! Police!"

Police! All I could think of was how mad Putnam was going to be!

chapter
SIX

"*En garde!*"

"Hey, run that reel again, will you?" I requested of my brain. My brain obliged. In slow motion.

First there was Ingrid screaming and the corpse behind me on the couch. Then there was the rustle from behind the couch as the figure popped up to grab the second fencing foil from the wall. Then there was Ingrid high-tailing it into the other room as the sword-wielding figure lunged for me.

"*En garde!*" he said.

"Got it now?" my brain wanted to know. "Got it!" I assured my brain. "*En garde!*" I echoed aloud, blocking the lunge with my own foil. For a moment, my adversary and I were locked together, blade to blade, staring into each others faces.

Oh, no! It was that mirror again. My fellow duelist was the crud with my face!

"Haven't I seen this movie before?" I asked my brain. "Shut up and keep dueling," my brain replied. "Douglas Fairbanks, wasn't it?" I persisted. "Senior, or Junior, I'm not sure which. Or maybe it was Louis Hayward, or

Ronald Colman. Zenda? One of the Dumas things?" My brain grew grumpy. "You can write Archer Winsten and ask him—if you live!" it told me nastily. "*Touche!*" I said aloud as my foe neatly sliced off my necktie.

"My compliments. You duel very well," my double saluted me.

"I took a merit badge in fencing when I was a Boy Scout," I told him truthfully. "I guess you never forget."

He cocked an ear toward the babble of voices approaching from the other side of the curtain. "They're bound to interrupt our duel, so I must kill you quickly, fool!" he said, rhyming. "Thrust home!" His blade lunged for my throat.

My throat lunged out of its way. So quickly, indeed, that I sprained my Adam's Apple executing the maneuver. "Ha! You missed, play actor!" I taunted him.

"We shall meet again!" he assured me, diving out the window as the crowd poured into the room.

"Sooner than you think, play actor," I retorted, following on his heels.

I half expected to land in a moat, but I didn't. We were on the ground floor, and what I landed in was a garbage pail. I jumped free of it and chased my double up the alley. It was a dead end. He turned, and we resumed our duel under the stars. A couple of alley cats watched without too much interest.

Thrust and counter-thrust; our blades danced an intricate ballet to the click-clack and pang-ping sounds of steel on steel. Sword-point twirled delicately about sword-point in the tickling movements of Death seeking an opening. Like acrobats we bounced and parried back up the alley to the street, down the street to the next alley, and through it to the next, and then the next.

Finally we stood fast in an alleyway between two old law tenements, barely habitable relics which had somehow been overlooked when the other dwellings had been torn down to make way for the buildings of commerce. A light sprang up behind a fire escape running up the wall of one of the buildings. It was like a movie projector casting our shadows—giant shadows—over white sheets hanging from a clothesline strung between the tenements. More lights dotted the scene, and an audience gathered to watch the enlarged shadow-duel.

My adversary hummed something Rudolph Frimml-y, and our foils clanged together in an intricate duet to pick up the beat. We held the note of the final chorus with the blades locked together, our knuckles almost grazing, teeth flashing white in the mirror image of each other's faces. "Well done, play actor," I complimented him.

"And I salute you," he replied.

We broke the impasse. Each fell back a step, and then resumed fencing.

"What's goin' on?" a voice inquired from one of the windows above us.

"Some kinda rumble, I think," another voice answered.

"Ain't it awful, the violence in the streets today?"

"They ain't in the street; they're in the alley."

"Man, aren't those the longest switchblades you ever saw?"

My foe executed a quick *entrechat*, landed sideways, and lunged for me. I was too quick for him. I slipped under his blade, and my sword-point was a flash of lightning striking the hilt of his weapon. It went spinning from his grip to the pavement. He dived for it, but he was too late. My foot pinned the blade to the ground, and my sword was at his throat, warning him away from it. He backed off, spreading his hands in a gesture of futility. I flicked my rapier and sent his foil flying through the air toward him, hilt-first. He caught it and bowed to acknowledge my chivalry.

"You are a true sportsman, sir." He paid tribute to my gallantry.

"I'm just a nice guy," I replied.

"But nice guys," he reminded me, "finish last!"

He punctuated the remark with a furious assault that backed me to the wall. I was forced to leap to the top of a garbage pail to avoid the frenzied stabbing of his blade. It whistled under my heels as I jumped.

"Five bucks says the guy with half a necktie loses."

"What odds?"

"No odds. They're an even match."

"Yeah, they're an even hatch."

"Now that ya mention it, there is a decided resemblance."

"Any takers?"

"Okay. I'll take five."

We were on the first-floor fire escape now. I was using the lid from a garbage pail to ward off my adversary's bloodthirsty blade. An intricate Graustarkian rhythm echoed between the buildings as his flailing sword ricocheted off my tin shield. His mouth was half cavalier smile, half snarl as he closed in on me.

"What did you do to Hortense?" I inquired as I fended him off.

"Nothing she didn't enjoy," he assured me as he feinted for my belly and then thrust for my throat.

"You fiend!" I defended myself with the garbage-can lid.

"Not at all. The damsel was flattered at your interest in her." He grabbed for my shield and we grappled for it.

"*My* interest?"

"Yes. Naturally Milady thought that I was you."

"What a heinous deception!"

"Nonsense! Believe me, you outdid yourself with her."

"You go too far!" My blade lunged for his grin, but he danced back out of range.

"You should be grateful to me. I've enhanced your reputation tremendously." His free hand was tugging at my shield again.

"You are lacking in ethics, sir!" I was panting from the struggle.

"Granted." He wrenched the garbage-pail lid from my grasp and sent it flying into the alley.

The maneuver took me off balance. I was forced to scamper up the fire escape to avoid his fury. I took my stand on the third-floor level and counterattacked. "How did you happen to get to the Swedish place, anyway?" I demanded.

"One thing leads to another." It was a cryptic slash.

"I thought you fooled Elsa and Barry into taking you and Hortense to a discipline club." I lunged.

"They were most obliging." He parried.

"I suppose it's no use asking you what you found out there." My blade executed a figure eight.

"No use at all." He reversed the figure, and once again we were at an impasse.

"Six-five says No-Tie takes him." The voice came from a head craned upward from a window beneath us.

"You're on."

I launched a spirited series of lunges against my double, and he turned tail. My final thrust pierced the seat of his pants. "*Touche!*" He jumped.

"*Touche?*" inquired a voice above us.

"He means 'tooshy'," a second voice explained. "That's where No-Tie got him."

"*Touche*, hell!" the Russian exclaimed. "That hurt!" He fled up the fire escape and turned as he reached the rooftop to meet my pursuit. "Farewell!" he shouted, and sent his sword hurtling at me point first.

I had to throw myself aside and downward to avoid

being struck by it. The hilt bounced against the side of the building with enough force so that the weapon ricocheted through the air and disappeared through an open window across the alley. Immediately, a masculine scream of pain sounded from the open window.

"Yoicks! My husband must be back!" A female voice chimed in with the man's scream. "You've got to get out of here!"

They were visible now. She was trying to push him onto the fire escape. He was having difficulty getting over the windowsill because of the sword protruding like a metal tail from his naked rear end. "Pull it out!" he begged.

"Hurry up and get out of here!" she insisted.

I left them to their problem as I swung up over the roof-ledge to continue my pursuit of my adversary. He was nowhere in sight. It was as if the night had swallowed him up. I dashed to the other side of the roof.

He was already three-quarters of the way down the fire escape on the other side of the building. I started after him, but it was no use. He paused for a brief instant as he reached the ground. "'Til we meet again, Mr. Victor," he called, mocking me with a deep, sweeping bow.

"'Til we meet again, play actor," I responded, bowing back and almost falling off the fire escape in the process.

His laughter continued to mock me as the blackness swallowed him up. I continued to the ground and decided the hell with it. There was no way of telling which way he'd gone. I'd had enough musketeering for one night, anyway. I decided to go back to my hotel and grab some shuteye.

I woke up with both arms full of pulchritude. Because of the breasts wrapped around my face, I was having difficulty breathing. I managed to extricate myself from

82

them and saw that the grayness of late afternoon was closing in on my hotel room.

"Oh! But you are a sleepyhead, darling. Did I knock you out that much? I suppose I should be flattered."

"I suppose so," I echoed unthinkingly as my bleary eyes struggled to focus on Hortense. There were still a few wisps of her red hair straggling over them, which made it difficult.

"Well, I feel the same way," she cooed. "My whole body aches. But it's delicious. Every time I move, I want to groan. But then I think of you and I want to sing. It really was wonderful, wasn't it?"

"Wonderful." I couldn't think of any reason not to agree.

"Absolutely extra-special."

"Absolutely." I was having trouble returning her tender glance. "Uh, how come you decided to drop in on me?"

"When you didn't call, I got worried." She looked just a little bit hurt. "You don't mind my coming over, do you?"

"Oh, no! Not at all. Glad to see you."

"I'm relieved." She beamed. "I was afraid you might think I was being over-possessive."

"Perish the thought." I struggled free of her embrace. "But I would appreciate it if you'd let me get a little air into my lungs."

"Oh, I'm sorry. I guess I just want to hug you forever. I'm afraid to let you go. I know it's foolish."

"I'm sure you have every right—"

"Oh! You still feel the same." She clapped her hands. "I'm so glad! I was afraid that in the cold light of morning—"

"Afternoon," I corrected her. "The cold light of afternoon."

"Afternoon," she agreed. "Anyway, I was afraid it

83

might just have been the evening's madness and you'd regret the things you said."

"I never regret anything I say," I assured her. *But I didn't say them,* I hedged mentally.

"I never thought anything so wonderful could happen to me, Steve," Hortense was positively glowing. "I mean, I'm not stupid. I know what I am. A tramp. I've never kidded myself. I never thought any man could fall in love with somebody who's done the things I've done. Men just don't fall in love with girls in my business."

"You're too hard on yourself."

"Oh, you aré so doggone sweet! But what I'm trying to explain is that it's not just that a man could feel that way about me. It's that I could fall in love with a man, too. You get pretty cynical about men when you're in the profession. Experience makes you that way. You don't figure to go for a guy seriously. You tell yourself there's nothing new under the ceiling. And then, out of the blue —last night! Wow! I still can't believe it's happening to me!"

"I can't believe it's happening to me, either!" I told Hortense fervently.

"Oh, I love you so much!"

I went down in a sea of kisses. "Just hold it a minute, will you, sweetie?" I gasped, fighting my way to the surface. "Maybe we should compare notes on what happened last night."

"What do you mean?" Her voice was a trifle trembly.

"Now, don't get upset. All I want to do is get the sequence of events straight for the survey."

"But you were there!"

"It's just a sort of cross-check," I told her weakly. "I want to see if our recollections jive. Just go through the evening from the beginning for me, will you?"

"It seems awfully silly."

"Do it for me, baby." I patted her.

"All right. I'll humor you if that's what you want. Oh, darling, there isn't anything I wouldn't do for you after last night. I'm hooked, that's what. I'm hooked on love. I'm hooked on you."

"That's my girl. Now start at the beginning."

"All right." She shrugged. "After you called me, I got dressed and you picked me up at my place. We took a cab over to pick up Barry and Elsa and—"

"Do you happen to remember where they live?"

"Why? Don't you? You had the address."

"I lost it."

"Oh. Well, it was just the other side of the river. Remember? Eucalyptus Drive. I don't remember the number, but I'd know the house if I saw it again."

"Good. Go on. What happened then?"

"Barry said you should pay off the cab and we'd take his car. The four of us piled into it, and he drove us back into Washington to the spank-party."

"Tell me everything that happened there."

"You mean while we were split up? But I already—"

"Everything. When we were together, too. Describe it all. I know it seems foolish, but I want to confirm all my recollections."

"Oh, all right." She shrugged off her puzzlement. "Barry parked the car in the lot behind this mansion he said used to be some kind of embassy building. We all went up on a veranda in back there, and this attendant in livery right out of Bismarck ushered us inside, clicking his heels like Prussian castanets. Barry introduced us to our host, Herr Von Koerner. You remember him, don't you?"

"Never mind what I remember. Go on."

"Well, Von Koerner was dressed formally, white tie and tails. I remember I had a hard time not giggling, he was such a stereotype. Bald, a scar on his cheek, jaw stuck out like a Panzer attack, even a monocle—it was too

85

much. And that riding crop he was carrying and kept thwacking against the palm of one hand—that was really the end. There he was, the Hun with *Kultur*, the Prussian turned Gestapo agent, leering formality all set for an evening of minor atrocities—he looked like one of those Grade C propaganda movies Hollywood used to turn out during the Second World War, the kind you see on the Late Show and think to yourself that the character would be ludicrous if not for the fact that his real-life counterparts were much worse. Anyway, when we were introduced, you spoke to him in German, and that impressed him. I could see that he took to you right away. I didn't know you could speak German so fluently, Steve."

"Neither did I," I muttered to myself.

"What?" When I didn't answer, Hortense continued. "Well, Herr Von Koerner introduced us around, and then—"

"About how many people were there would you say?" I interrupted.

"Oh, a dozen, I guess, besides the four of us."

"Girls and boys?"

"What else is there? Never mind, I withdraw the question. Yes, it was split evenly. But you know that! I really don't see why—"

"I'm a kook! Okay? Now please, Honey, go on."

"Ooh! When you call me *Honey* like that, I go all shivery. Can you imagine? A girl with my experience? Ridiculous, isn't it?"

"Yes, it is."

"Steve!"

"Sorry. I'm sorry. I was only kidding. Honest. Now will you please get on with it?"

"Well, all right." Her tone said she was only half mollified. "Von Koerner served us some light wine, and then the entertainment began."

"Entertainment?"

"More like a calculated warm-up, I guess. Prussian precision. Remember? Barry called them the Reichstag Rockettes. Six Brunhilds right out of Wagner, all got up with those idiotic breastplates and the Viking helmets, with their bare bottoms sticking out and their muscles bulging when they snapped those whips. It was like a military drill with choreography by the Marquis de Sade. And the precise way they lashed each other! It was too much—a Hitlerian sadist's version of the Easter spectacle at the Radio City Music Hall. And that finale!"

"Yeah, it was really something. Describe it to me, though, in case I missed something."

"The three girls lashing out at the other three in unison, just the perfectly timed six strokes, and then the reverse, until all six *derrieres* were crisscrossed with those thin lines of blood forming six perfect swastikas."

"Swastikas? I'll be damned!"

"That's how I felt. It gave me the chills. But you explained to me that under the circumstances it didn't have any political significance, and I felt better."

"I did explain that, huh?"

"Yes. You even wisecracked about how with a little training the girls might learn to carve out the design of a hammer and sickle."

"I didn't know I dared indulge in such heresies."

"What?"

"Never mind. Go on with the story."

"Well, after that we had a little more wine, and then we began pairing off. Von Koerner had taken a fancy to me, and so I was his little whipping boy—his phrase, not mine, and make of it what you will, Dr. Freud—for the evening. I lost track of Elsa and Barry. You were corraled by a hefty blonde type name of Gretchen, I believe. I guess some men go for that sort of obvious female with too much of everything. I don't see why, though. They're so terribly obvious. There's nothing subtle about their appeal. Your friend Gretchen was waving those mammaries and hips of hers around like they were a red flag and you were a bull whose attention she was trying to attract. You did mean it when you said later that she disgusted you, didn't you, Steve?" Hortense was anxious.

"Absolutely," I assured her. "Go on. Tell me what happened with Von Koerner."

"Are you sure you won't find it painful, dear? I mean, now that we've discovered what we mean to each other—"

"I'll grit my teeth."

"No, darling, really—"

"It's all right," I assured her. "I'm a big boy now. I promise not to be jealous."

"All right then. He took me upstairs to his little room and he made me pull my skirt up. Then he pulled my bloomers down."

"Bloomers? I didn't know girls wore bloomers any more."

"I'm an old-fashioned girl," Hortense told me demurely. "Anyway, then he made me bend over across his lap and he spanked me."

"With his bare hand?"

"Yes. He kept calling me his naughty baby and his bad girl and things like that, and he really laid it on. I tell you, he kept it up until it was really swollen a bright red."

"How could you tell?"

"Mirrors. They were all over the place. I could see every part of me and of him. As a matter of fact, I could see my poor backside in triplicate all the time he was punishing me. I tell you, Steve, in my business I've made some wild scenes, but this was really bizarre."

"Bizarre how?"

"Well, while he was spanking me, I naturally assumed he was leading up to sex. I mean, I've known sadists before. Stretched over his lap that way, I could feel him getting excited and I figured that sooner or later we'd get to it. But he didn't swing quite that way. He was even further out than I'd suspected. He wasn't working up to sex plain and simple, but to more kooky discipline."

"Like what?"

"Like when I began yelling 'Uncle!' he started us on the next phase. My pain excited him. But it excited him so that he wanted to feel pain himself, not so that he wanted sex with me right away. He made me stand up. He tucked my skirt up around my waist so that I was naked from the hips down. Then he took off his pants, took off the belt, and handed it to me. He wrapped both fists around himself, and then bent over so that I could beat him with the belt."

"And you obliged?"

"Why not? Better him than me." Hortense was realistic about it. "Besides, by that time I was feeling some hostility of my own. My *derriere* was pretty damn sore from his smacking it and pinching it. To tell the truth, I kind of liked the idea of getting my licks in. Even if he enjoyed it, the way I was feeling, he deserved it."

"Understandable," I assured her.

"Yes. Well, I laid it on with the belt, and that nut kept saying 'Harder! Harder!' until my arm was getting tired. He let me rest for a minute, and then he showed me how to use the belt so that the metal buckle would cut him when I struck. I did what he wanted, and that really sent him into ecstasy. Both his hands were going on all eight cylinders, and he just kept getting bigger and bigger. Watching him grow, I began to be afraid then that he would want sex. I'm built pretty normally myself—as you know, darling—and I knew that this outsize Prussian would really hurt me. But that still wasn't what he wanted."

"What did he want?"

"Wait. You'll see. He made me sit in this armchair,

and then he sat on my lap, facing me. Then he made me slap him across the face with the belt—just the leather part, not the buckle. And then he said I should tell him what a bad boy he was and how he deserved to be punished. 'Nein, *Mutter! Bitte, Mutter! Nein! Mutter! Mutter! Mutter!*' He kept protesting and carrying on that way. But he didn't want me to stop. When I tried, he got angry, and so I kept on humoring him. Finally, he was on the verge. Then came the sickest part of all."

"What was that?"

"He stood up. There was this end table beside the chair —just the right height. He put it down on the end table and it was immense. Honestly, Steve, you can't imagine—"

"When I laid that thing on old Joe's bar/ I'll sw'ar it stretched from thar to thar," I quoted.

"Exactly! Only farther. Anyway, then he reached over and unbuttoned the front of my dress and pushed it down. He pushed my bra down, too. Then he took both his hands with the fingers sort of formed into two sets of pincers, and, using just the tips, he squeezed my nipples. He squeezed very hard, and I let out a yell. He liked that, the bastard! He said why didn't I fight back, and he took time out to show me what he meant. He wanted me to slam my fist down on that monster of his on the end table. Well, when he pinched the tips of my breasts again, I did it, all right. I pounded it with a vengeance."

"Ouch!" I couldn't help emphathizing.

"He kept pinching—a sort of delicate, exquisite torture—and I kept hitting it as hard as I could, over and over again. That really got to him. He went at me with his teeth then. Just nibbling the tips, but with sharp pressure so that it really hurt. I actually became afraid he'd bite them off. But I was mad, too. I guess I sort of got carried away with the situation despite myself. I began clawing him, really gouging with all five fingers."

"You mean his—?"

"Yep! I really ripped away at it."

"Phew!" I shuddered. "Didn't that cure his lust?"

"On the contrary, if anything it got to him even more. He made me beat a tattoo on it with both hands then. I hit it as hard as I could, but still he kept insisting I hit harder. Finally, he grabbed me here"—Hortense pointed —"with all five fingers, and almost turned me inside out. I yelled and came down on it with all my might. That did it. The result was all over the wall on the other side of the room."

"You mean the two of you didn't—?"

"Nope. He didn't want sex. He wanted it beaten out of him. And once I'd obliged, he seemed to just lose interest in me completely. He was so brusque he was positively rude when he took me back to rejoin the others."

"Was I there?"

"Of course you were, darling. And you were so sympathetic and tender. I'll never forget it. You made me feel like a little girl who'd hurt herself instead of a professional whore. Of course, you did ask a lot of questions. But then you're always asking questions. You are the darnedest man that way. I swear, darling, if I didn't love you so much, I'd really be annoyed."

"What sort of questions did I ask?"

"There you go again!"

"Please, Hortense. It's important."

"I don't see why. After all, you asked them. I don't understand why you want me to tell you what you said to me. It's silly!"

"Please."

"Oh, all right. Earlier you'd asked me to pump him about a couple named Cromwell, or a girl named Carrie. Now you wanted to know what I'd found out."

"And what had you found out?"

"Nothing. Only that Von Koerner said he knew the girl. That was all."

"That's enough."

"That's what you said last night. And I still don't know what you mean."

"Forget it."

"I don't know." Hortense was suspicious. "Who is this Carrie Cromwell anyway? You carrying a torch for her or something? You kept trying to pump Barry and Elsa about her, too."

"Did I get anywhere?" I ignored Hortense's jealousy.

"Only that we're going back with them to Von Koerner's again in a few days because maybe she'll be there."

I decided that was one event in which my Russian double wasn't going to sub for me. "What else happened at Von Koerner's?" I asked aloud.

"Nothing. You went into a huddle with that Gretchen for a minute, which I didn't like, and then we left."

"With Elsa and Barry?"

"No. We took a cab by ourselves to my place. Some ride!" She giggled. "You were all over me. But you kept asking all those questions between every kiss. I guess I'll have to get used to that. Everybody has his idiosyncrasies."

"I'll just bet I asked questions," I mused. "What did we do then?"

"Now don't tell me you don't remember *that!*" Hortense actually blushed—no mean feat, considering how blush-proof her career should have made her.

"Oh, sure. It was great." I glossed over it.

"That it was. But over too soon. Why did you have to rush away that way?"

"Didn't I say why?"

"A business appointment, you said. But in the middle of the night?"

"That's the kind of business I'm in."

"Well, it wasn't very flattering. But I must admit I was on Cloud Nine, so I guess I didn't mind too much. I didn't mind anything after what you said to me just before you left."

"What did I say?" I asked automatically.

"Oh, please, Steve! Ask me all the ridiculous questions you want about last night, but don't tell me you forgot that. Oh, you couldn't have! After you said my past didn't matter and everything. After you made me believe how wonderful it could be. And you said we'd do it day after tomorrow. Remember?"

"Do what day after tomorrow?"

"Get married!" she wailed. "You asked me to marry you and I accepted. You just couldn't forget a thing like that, Steve!"

"Get married?" I was dazed.

"You even told me to wire my mother to come for the wedding."

"Get married?"

"Yes, darling. Oh, you're just still half-asleep, that's all. I'm going to make you such a good wife! But right now I'm going to run out and buy some things for the wedding. A white bridal dress and a black nightgown. How does that sound, darling?"

"Get married?"

"Call me later." Hortense blew me a kiss and she was gone.

Get married? If I ever got my hands on that sadistic, traitorous, atrocity-committing Russian "pre-vert," I'd— Some place in the back of my mind, a funeral organ played a Volgalike version of Lohengrin in dirge-time. *Married!!!*

chapter
SEVEN

"*Rape?*"

"Rape!" I repeated wearily.

"Now see here, Mr. Victor, this is too much!" Putnam's voice crackled in the telephone receiver like a sputtering fuse about to explode.

"It's not my fault."

The cop standing beside me at the precinct desk snorted.

"It's never your fault. First murder, then assault, then another murder after I expressly warned you how important Hajstrom was, and now this!"

"I'd been meaning to give you a ring and explain about about that Hajstrom business, but—"

"Explain! I suppose you're going to tell me you didn't kill him, either!"

"I didn't."

"Then who did? Your twin brother?"

"You're getting warm."

"I can see where it's pretty handy having a double to blame for everything, Mr. Victor. I suppose this rape business is his fault, too."

"Well, in a way it is."

"I'll just bet! And tell me, Mr. Victor, just who is your victim this time?"

"Well, she's not exactly a victim. And certainly not mine. It's Helen Quentin's sister, Patricia."

"That little girl!"

I looked at Patricia powdering her nose on the other side of the police station. Her sweater was torn and one of her upthrust adolescent breasts seemed about to spring free of it. What was left of her short-shorts stretched tight over her buttocks, and she smiled smugly into the mirror of the compact as she caught one of the cops eyeing her. "She's not such a little girl," I told Putnam.

"That's no excuse! You should be ashamed of yourself, Victor. The statutory rape laws are specifically designed to protect minors."

"The rape I'm accused of isn't statutory."

"Do you mean that you actually forced—?"

"I didn't! But that's what I'm accused of. And you'd better hustle down here and get me off the hook before they lock up your prize I-spy and throw away the key."

Putnam took a deep breath to restrain himself. "Suppose you tell me just exactly what happened, Mr. Victor."

"I can't over the phone," I told him. "It's a very complicated story . . ."

That it was. It all began that afternoon after my would-be bride left my hotel room. A cold shower unstunned me, and an early dinner started my thought processes grinding again. A few Scotches at a bar around the corner from the hotel jogged them into high gear. Still, I was running strictly on questions. Like—

What was the connection between the spank-club my Russian double had visited with Hortense and the disappearance of the Cromwells? Did this Von Koerner figure

95

into it? What about Gretchen, the over-endowed blonde the Russian had played games with in my name? Had she provided any leads to the whereabouts of the Cromwells? Had she steered him to the Swedish peekaboo parlor? If not, how had my murderous look-alike found the place? And having found it, why had he killed Hajstrom? What was the connection between Hajstrom and Ingrid? Had Hajstrom perhaps been looking for Cromwell on his own? Had Ingrid provided him with any leads? Why did he . . . ? Why did she . . . ? Why did they . . . ? Why? Why? Why . . . ? Why was I born . . . ? Why am I living . . . ?

I hit the brake, and my mind skidded to a halt. Some questions are just arrows of frustration pointing the way to the laughing academy. And others only time can answer. The ones about the spank-party and Von Koerner and Gretchen all seemed to fall in the second category. That left me with Hajstrom and Ingrid. Being slightly dead, Hajstrom was in a lousy position to provide me with any answers. So I parked alongside of Ingrid and dropped in some change.

The phone booth was stuffy as I dialed. My ear buzzed three times before Helen Quentin answered. Why Helen Quentin? Well, I didn't have Ingrid's number, or her last name either for that matter—that's why. Sometimes the long way around is the only way.

"Steve Victor here." I identified myself.

"What do you want?" There was fear in Helen's voice, which didn't exactly make her sound glad to hear from me.

"I want to get in touch with Ingrid. I thought you might be able to give me her last name and phone number."

There was a long pause. Then— "Why do you want that?" She sounded even more afraid, and I realized that she was probably bugged because she thought I might tell Ingrid about finding Phil with her the night before.

"Nothing to do with you." I tried to reassure her. "It's strictly business. I want to ask her some questions about the 'Friends of Sweden.' It's for O. R. G. Y. All very confidential."

"I don't think she'd want me to give you any information about her."

"I don't want you to give me any information about her. I just want you to tell me how to get in touch with her."

"She might not like that, either."

"There's a lot of things she might not like if she knew about them." I squeezed a little.

Helen thought that over. "You're right," she acknowledged finally. "Still I don't think I should tell you those things. But," she added hastily, "perhaps I can make some other arrangement that might satisfy you. That is if you'll promise to be discreet about last night."

"What arrangement?" When she didn't answer, I added an assurance that I'd be suffering lockjaw where she and Phil were concerned.

"You can talk to Ingrid over here. At my place."

"When?"

"Oh, say in an hour. She's coming over to spend the evening with me."

"*Sans* Phil," I guessed.

"Right. And that's something else you have to promise not to mention. Anyway, not to Phil. He's very jealous where I'm concerned."

"Tell me," I said, "how do you figure to find the time to bury George?"

"Don't be sarcastic. It's unseemly—particularly since you murdered him."

"I did not murder him!"

97

"I saw you do it. Remember? Which reminds me, there's something I'd very much like to ask you. Since I'm doing you this favor with Ingrid, will you promise to give me an honest answer?"

"I'll do my best."

"Did my family put you up to murdering George?" Helen wanted to know.

"Not that I know of," I told her. "But why do you ask? Didn't they approve of Georgie-porgie?"

"No. They were convinced I married beneath us. Impoverished aristocracy, you know? And somehow Dad got wind of our little parties. He wrote me he was disowning me—which was a laugh, considering that he hasn't got a red cent to deny me in his will. He's also sore because of Pat. He wants her to come home. But she won't go, and I don't see any reason why I should make her. Do you?"

"Nope. I think your home's a good, healthy heterosexual environment for any adolescent girl."

"There you go being sarcastic again. And you didn't give me a straight answer to my question, either. Was Dad behind George's murder? I wouldn't put it past him. He has the most warped concept of family honor you can imagine. Besides, if he didn't put you up to it, who did? I can't think of anyone else who'd want poor George killed."

"My guess is it was an accident," I told her. "George wasn't meant to be murdered. He just couldn't stand up under the gaff. I don't think his death was planned."

"Your guess! Why do you put it that way? Who else would know why you murdered George if you don't?"

"I told you, I didn't murder him!"

"Oh! If you aren't the most infuriating man! I don't care what anybody does. We all make mistakes. None of us is perfect. But at least be man enough to own up to it. You don't have to lie about it."

"I'm not lying. I did not kill your husband. Period."

"Oh, all right! Be a hypocrite! George may have had his faults, but at least *he* never lied!"

"I'll see you and Ingrid in an hour," I told her, ending the conversation.

I stopped back at my hotel for a quick shave before leaving for the Quentin home. As I was on my way out again, the desk clerk hailed me. There was a message for me. It was from Hortense. She had called to ask for my mother's address so she could invite her to the wedding.

"She said if you went out again, would you please leave it with me, sir," the desk clerk told me politely. "The lady said she would call back later."

"Tell her not to bother about the address," I instructed him. "Tell her my mother won't come in any case. She's Orthodox."

"Yes, sir. Orthodox, sir. Shall I mention any particular faith, sir?"

"Zoroastran. And you might add that she's violently opposed to mixed marriages."

"Yes, sir. I'll tell the young lady when she calls, sir. And, sir—" He called as I started away from the desk.

"Yes?" I turned to look at him.

"Might I extend heartiest congratulations and best wishes from myself and the hotel management, sir?"

"Drop dead!" As I went through the lobby door, his jaw was still hanging open.

My own jaw was clenched with fury as I thought about the diabolical Russian who'd gotten me into this mess. All through the cab ride out to Helen Quentin's house, I occupied my mind by inventing tortures for him. He was in the process of being drawn and quartered when the taxi discharged me at my destination.

I walked up to the front door. There was a note tacked there. It was for me.

Mr. Victor:

Have gone to pick Ingrid up as Phil is using their car tonight. Back in about a half-hour or so. Suggest you wait in the gardens around back as they're very pleasant at this time of year.

Helen Quentin

So I strolled around to the back of the house where the gardens were. Helen hadn't been bragging about them. The landscaping really was very pleasant. Every inch of the half-acre of land the house perched on had been carefully manicured. And while the landscaping was colorful and intricate, it was in excellent taste.

From the patio there extended a very green, neatly trimmed lawn bordered by a series of flower beds. High hedges fenced off the flower beds. Three or four flagstone paths led off from them. One of the paths led to a grove of fruit trees, another to a circular area defined by smaller trees blooming with Japanese cherry blossoms. Stately oaks lined a third path which led to still more hedges forming a sort of intricate maze. There were fountains and rock gardens and statuary and still more flower beds—tulips predominating—sprinkled about the property. More high dense hedges shielded the Quentin land from the street beyond.

I wandered about idly, admiring the artistry, the work and planning, which had been put into the grounds. Reaching the grove of fruit trees, I stopped to admire a particularly tall pear tree. Its branches, ripe fruit hanging from them, were gnarled and twining with an intricate upward sweep. It was a tree just made for climbing.

Feeling a little silly, I pulled myself up to the first crisscrossed bower of branches and reached for a particularly juicy-looking pear. As I stretched for it, my head craned upward and I saw that there was a sort of platform and tree-house in the branches above me. Bemused, I just had to climb up for a closer look at it.

It was even larger and more complex than it had seemed from below. The platform was about eight feet square and extended beyond that area to a sort of little thatched hut. I entered the hut and smiled at the ingenuity of it. Following the line of the tree trunk, it had been built up so that there was a ladder leading to a second level where there was another platform which had been covered to form a sort of turret. This area was large enough for two people to sit side by side comfortably. There was a sort of metal pipe on hinges attached to the outer "wall"—really an arrangement of fronds and branches. I examined it and found an eyepiece from a telescope attached to it.

Looking through the eyepiece, I found that I had a clear view of the ground below. The metal pipe evidently ran all the way down the tree with mirrors arranged inside it so that it was a sort of periscope in reverse. It could be turned so that it provided a sweeping view of the area beyond the base of the tree. I swiveled it, chuckling to myself with delight, and feeling like Tom Sawyer.

Jimminy Cricket! Or whatever the hell it was those clean-living lads of the Tom Sawyer era used to exclaim when Farmer Brown caught them in the apple orchard. Whatever it was, I substituted a pithier expression as I peered through the upside-down scope and spotted two figures among the fruit trees. They were heading straight for the one I was in, the one with the tree-house. A moment later they were out of sight as they began climbing up the pear tree.

I hugged the shadows of the upper level of the tree-house and peered down through the hole in the flooring

101

which admitted the ladder. After a moment or two I saw them climbing onto the wide lower platform. I shrank even farther back as I saw who it was.

It was Patricia, Helen Quentin's fifteen-year-old kid sister. She was one of the last people I wanted to run into at the moment. She was convinced I'd killed George. She thought she'd seen me do it. I had no desire to face the hysteria I was sure my presence would evoke from her.

The boy with her was familiar to me. I'd seen him before, that night Helen had given me my French lesson. He was the boy who'd been making out with Patricia while they were ostensibly watching TV. I remembered that Helen had called him "Leonard."

Leonard was a gangly lad, perhaps a year or two older than Patricia. Brown hair, long in back, cut Beatle-style in front, accentuated an Elvis Presley jawline (or lack of it) that lent his fat-lipped, slack features a feeling of dull-wittedness which fit in with the seeming lack of coordination of his floppy limbs. For all that, though, his arms were bulgy with muscles beneath the short, rolled-up sleeves of the T-shirt he wore. All in all, Leonard looked like a strong, not-too-bright farm boy who'd run into a barber with a penchant for practical jokes.

Just on looks alone, Patricia seemed far more mature than he did. She had the body of a woman—fully developed breasts, firm, ample hips, filled-out and shapely legs—and when she moved around, she moved them like the body of a woman. Her hair was blonder than her sister's and she wore it in a ponytail. Her face was heart-shaped, with even features and slanted green eyes that made it look both feminine and feline. There was intuitive knowledge and sexuality in those eyes, a sort of subtle hipness that put her years ahead of Leonard and said she was sure of her ability to wrap him—or any male —around her pinky finger. Her make-up was the only childish thing about her. It was inch-thick and green around the eyes, and her lipstick was a fluorescent shade of greenish gold like tarnished brass. Pound for pound, in the short-shorts and sweater she was wearing, she could have given Lolita a run for her money. Indeed, with her attributes and youthful energy, she looked well able to out-lure any of the more mature love goddesses currently reigning over the silver screen.

They'd settled onto the outside part of the platform below me now. I couldn't see them too well. But I could hear them clearly. Leonard was strumming a guitar. After a moment he began to sing. At least I think it was meant to be singing. What it sounded like was a tomcat with a bad case of adenoids in the process of being altered. To put it more kindly, as a modern troubador serenading his lady, Leonard was a bit too nasal for my taste. But then every man (or boy) to his own mating call! His went something like this:

"Nobody understan-an-an-an-an-an-an-an-ands—
"Me!
"No-no-no-nobody understan-an-ands—
"Me!
"Pop say be a man-an-an-an-an-an-an-an-an—
"Boy!
"Ma say do it if you can-an-an-an-an-an-an—
"Boy!"
"Teach say better have a plan-an-an-an-an—
"Boy!
"Else you'll be duckin' lead in Vietnam-am-am—
"Boy!
"Nobody, no, nobody understan-an-an-an-an-an-ands—
"Me!
"Ain't nobody dig, nor understan-an-ands—
"Me!
"Preacher, he say don't you kill-ill-ill—
"Boy!

"Ain't no way to get yourself a thrill-ill-ill—
"Boy!
"But you gotta go; it's Lyndon's will-ill-ill—
"Boy!
"On'y Godless Reds don' shoot they fill-ill-ill—
"Boy!
"No-bah-bah-bah-bah-body understan-an-ands—
"Me!
"No-no-no-no-no-body understan-an-ands—
"Me-me-me-me!
" 'Ceptin for my chick, she like me live—
"Boy!
"She don't dig Vietnam, nor all that jive—
"Boy!
"She say 'Make love, not war'; that how we strive—
"Boy!
"Better bed than dead's how we contrive—
"Boy!
"So-so-so-so-so-so—
"My baby understan-an-an-an-an-an-ands—
"Me!
"Yes-yes-yes-yes-yes-yes—
"At last somebody understan-an-ands—
"Me-ee-ee-ee-ee—ee—eeow!"

It was enough to turn a "dove" like me into a "hawk."
I took my fingers out of my ears just in time to hear Patricia speak.

"Leonard, that's the most touching melody I ever heard," she said. "Honestly, I'm all choked up!"

So was I, but with me it was the result of a rising gorge.

"And the lyric!" Patricia continued. "It really says it. You have a real talent, Leonard."

I shuddered for the future of show biz.

"Then you don't think it's too Dylan-y?" Leonard wanted to know.

"Not at all. It's fresh. In a way, it sort of reminds me of 'The Fugs'."

"Then you think it has cool?"

"Has it ever!"

"Thanks, Pat. I was afraid it might be just a little Camp."

"Camp!" She sneered the word. "You really low-rate yourself, Leonard. That song speaks for today. Camp's strictly from day-before-yesterday."

"Gee, Batman's still with it, Pat. That's Camp."

"Yeah, but it's also *jump*. That's why it's in. And that's why your song's an in-thing-sing. It's leap!"

"You really think so? You're not putting me on?"

"No, Leonard. It's hop! It's almost— Yes, it is! It's vault!"

"I don't know, I thought the second verse might be just a little bit on the plunge side. That bugged me."

"That's your inferiority complex talking, Leonard. It's not even high-dive, let alone gainer. I tell you, it's like really zoom!"

"Zoom?" Leonard sounded awed. "No kidding?"

"I wouldn't skid you. It really bounces it right in the faces of the leadfoots. It pulls the springs right out from under 'em. And what really gets me is it's so tender the pogo-sticks 'll bound right out of their kangaroo-jeans. You've just got to play it at the next frog-jump."

"Okay. I'm gambol."

These strange sounds were having a little trouble penetrating my varicose ears, but I kept listening anyway. Like they say, the world is for the young, communication is the problem, and you have to make the effort. That is, you have to make it if you don't want to be labeled a "crawl."

"How long did it take you to bounce it?" Patricia was asking.

"About three flips of the sand-jar. I ball-pointed it last

night. I was just yodelin' up the arrangement when my ancestors came in from some pit-party they were at. You should have heard the Papa-poke. Crawled all over the walls when he heard the jump-words. All that plaintive ooze about the fogey-neighbors an' how I'd offend their creep-spirit."

"I can imagine. All that 'shape-up-or-ship-out' grovel. My sister drips it on me all the time."

"How can they be so trudge?" Leonard sighed.

"It's 'cause they're tomb-age."

"That's no excuse. I'm never gonna pace like that. I'll jump 'til the day I bounce off the ball."

"Me too. That conformity squeeze isn't for me. I'll never dribble like that!" Patricia vowed.

"Hey," Leonard noticed, "that a new lipstick? It's real hurdle."

"Isn't it the living hop? All the girls are wearing it."

"Yeah. You know, what you were saying about conformity—you got it up pat. It really cuts my tendons how the huffers want we should all crawl alike and think alike and do everything the same. You ever ear-hop them? They even sound exactly the same when that grovel comes out of their craws."

"Yeah. It's like a different language."

"I'd rather sink than sound like that," Leonard said earnestly. "I don't know how they ever potsy each other."

"I guess when you're a crawl, you talk like a crawl and you potsy the other crawls, that's all."

"And how about the trudgy way they dress? Isn't that the living hop?"

"And how! All the button-down Papa-pokes and the slow-sack Mama-pokes. All looking the same. Poke-styles by General Motors, all oozing off the same assembly line. Conformity!"

"Yeah! Conformity!" Leonard agreed. "Hey, Pat, speaking of jump-suits," he added, "you should see the

106

leap toga-togs I raised the other day. Me and Hal and Grumble and Archie all bought the same spurt-jackets. Purple with a green check. We're gonna all wear 'em to school on the same day an ' watch the creep-teach hobble the ceiling. That'll show 'em they can't make us conform."

"It's the only way," Pat agreed earnestly. "Non-conformity isn't enough by itself. It has to be organized non-conformity. All us real jump kids getting together and being non-conformist at the same time in the same way. That's the only way not to conform."

"That's right. We've all got to not conform the same. We've got to get organized! Leapers of the world, unite!"

"Exactly! You've got nothing to lose but your stem-winders."

"Gee, Pat, it's real vault how we hop the same way about everything. Makes me feel like we got a real jump rapport."

"Flip off." Patricia sounded coy. "I've heard that countdown before. That's squeaky hop. You don't mean it."

"Sure I do. I've never been more high-jump in my life."

There was silence for a long moment. "Oh, Leonard," Patricia finally said breathlessly, "when you pucker me that way I just go all hoppity-hop inside."

"I'm hop. You really ricochet me too, baby." Leonard stretched. "Hey, you know, this is a real jump trampoline you got here. It's like real vault. Romantic, too."

"Mmm. It's a cozy bounce. Come on, I'll show you the inside."

I huddled back in the shadows as they entered the enclosed area beneath me. I could see them clearly now as Leonard leered at Patricia like an octopus and enveloped her in his eight adolescent arms. She responded like maybe eight wasn't enough.

"Pucker me again, Leonard."

Leonard obliged.

"Oh," she sighed when the kiss was over. "This isn't vault. You're getting all jumped up."

"Throbby-bounce!" he murmured.

"One-two-three-O'Lairy!" she sighed.

"I'm jump all over!" he groaned.

"Vault-vault-vault!" she panted.

"Hop-hop, baby. Hop-hop!" he groaned.

"Oh, Leonard, do you think we should? I'm afraid I'll get puff."

"Don't you take the prance-pills?"

"My sister wouldn't get them for me. You know how trudge she is."

"It's okay, bunny-frog. Don't worry. I'm a jump-scout. All prepared."

"Leonard, this is the first time I ever—"

I leaned over for a better view. Okay, so I'm a voyeur. Nobody's perfect. And how do you think I got to be the man from O.R.G.Y., anyway?

Patricia was stretched out on the floor of the treehouse. Leonard had pushed her sweater up over her shoulders. Her young breasts pointed up at me like two scarlet-beaked doves eager to be fed. Leonard was fumbling at her hips with the buttons of her shorts. His jeans were already down around his ankles. His adolescent lust was a murderous spear catching the moonlight. I revised my opinion as to his lack of maturity. Intellectually I might have been right, but physically he was a grown man-and-a-half.

Patricia was trembling with eagerness. As Leonard undid the buttons and fumbled inside her shorts, she threw her head back and gasped. Her eyes, green and bright and staring, looked straight up. And that was my undoing. They focussed straight on me. Patricia blinked once and screamed.

I scrambled to my feet, which was also a mistake. My

ankle turned under me. I skidded forward and found myself sliding down the ladder. For a minute the three of us rolled around inside the tree-house in an impossible tangle of arms and legs.

Finally I managed to tear loose and darted for the platform outside. Leonard dived for me and was tripped up by the jeans around his ankles. He managed to get a hand on me, though, and tripped me up. Patricia, her sweater still pushed up over her exposed breasts, had pulled a frond out of the tree-house wall and was flailing me over the head with it. "Murderer!" she screamed. "Murderer!"

Was dear old George never going to stop haunting me? I pondered the question as I tried to stave off the two of them. They'd backed me to the edge of the platform now. Leonard—wisely—paused to pull up his jeans. I took advantage of his preoccupation to start to climb down the tree. But Patricia wasn't willing to let bygones be bygones. "Murderer!" she screamed again, lunging for my face with long, well-honed nails.

Automatically I raised a hand to protect my precious profile. It latched onto Patricia's wrist. She was caught off balance, and her weight descended on me. The two of us went slipping and sliding through the branches of the tree together, finally landing on the ground below.

Her sweater and shorts were badly ripped by the fall. They were in tatters, and the tatters weren't doing much about covering her compact little body. One breast was exposed, and the opposite hip was sticking out nakedly in an interesting new style of bikini-wear. As I got to my feet, she backed away from me, still screaming like Fay Wray about to be Konged by the gorilla.

"Patricia. Are you all right?" Leonard called from above.

"Help!" she replied. "Murder! Help!"

"Look here." I tried to reason with her. "I'm not go-

109

ing to—" I broke off as I spied Leonard shinnying down the tree. He had what looked like a large club in one hand.

I bounced away. Yeah, I was real leap. I moved so fast, you might almost say I was vault!

The two jumps were one jump behind me. Youth was on their side. Their adrenal glands were definitely more hop than mine were. My mind recognized with a sigh that I was nothing but a crawl, and saw the impossibility of outdistancing them. The only leap thing to do was lose myself. So I made a beeline for the maze of hedges and managed to reach it before they could catch me.

The maneuver gave me a moment's respite. I could hear them thrashing around in the maze as I caught my breath. "You go this way; I'll go that way," I heard Patricia say.

"Do you think we should separate?" Leonard replied. "He might be dangerous."

"He is dangerous. He's a murderer. But don't worry, I'll yell if I see him."

Footsteps were getting closer now. I plunged deeper into the maze. As I turned and twisted through the hedges, I could appreciate how those rats must feel when they're subjected to this sort of experiment. It wasn't long before I had that real lost feeling, if you know what I mean.

There was no future there. That was for sure. I decided I'd better find my way out while Patricia and Leonard were still in the maze looking for me. But that was easier said than done. No matter which way I turned, I just seemed to get deeper into the complex of hedges. Then, to complicate my predicament, I heard footsteps approaching behind me.

I ran. The footsteps stayed right with me. No matter how I twisted and turned through the hedges, they seemed always right behind me. Then I made a sharp turn and fell right over Patricia.

"Murderer!" She screamed loud and long. "Help!" She started running away from me.

The footsteps were still behind me. Also, Leonard's voice: "Pat! Pat, where are you?" I had no choice but to run off in the same direction Patricia had taken.

"Leonard, he's chasing me!" she screamed over her shoulder.

"I'm coming, baby. Keep running."

She kept running. I kept running. He kept running. 'Round and 'round we went, Patricia in the lead, me behind her, Leonard somewhere behind me. Then Patricia took an unexpected turn, I followed her, and Leonard's footsteps receded behind us.

"Patricia?" he called plaintively. "Where are you, baby?"

"Murderer!" she hissed at me over her shoulder.

"You've got me wrong," I panted, but it was no use.

Patricia took another turn. Again I followed. Suddenly I found myself out of the maze. She was sprinting for a gate between the hedges at the edge of the Quentins' property. It wasn't that I was following her, but it did seem the logical way to go if I wanted to get out of this mess.

"Patricia?" Leonard's voice was a dim echo coming from the interior of the maze of hedges.

Patricia was through the gate now and out on the street. I followed.

"Help!" she called when she saw me appear. "Murder!" she called. "Police!" she bellowed.

I made the effort and caught up with her. "Now look here," I said. "I'm not going to hurt you. If you'll just stand still a minute—"

"Help!" She tried to pull away. Somehow my ankle got

111

between her feet, and she tripped and fell. She grabbed at me for support as she went down. Caught off balance myself, I fell on top of her.

"Help! Rape! Police! Rape!"

Wouldn't you know she'd have to pick that moment to change her tune? Hearing a car coming up the street, I tried to cover her mouth with my hand so she wouldn't be heard. She bit the hand and I jerked it away.

"Help! Rape!" she screamed again.

The car screeched to a halt at the curb. You guessed it. It was a police car. Two cops came bounding out with drawn pistols, dragged me off Patricia, and pulled me to my feet.

"Rape!" Patricia stammered incoherently.

The cops took in her torn clothing and the scratches and bruises she'd picked up during our wild gambol. Then they stared at my bleeding hand and disheveled clothing. "You degenerate bastard!" one of them said, slapping me open-handed across the face.

"He's a murderer, too," Patricia informed him helpfully.

"Whatta you got to say for yourself, you filthy creep?" the second cop asked.

"I'm not a creep," I told him wearily. "I'm hop. I'm skip. I'm jump all the way!"

Hell, if you want to play games with the kids, you have to speak their language, don't you? Isn't that the living hop?

chapter
EIGHT

"So YOU SEE," I finished explaining to Putnam, "far from raping this innocent young girl, I actually was responsible for preserving her virtue, for saving her from herself, from a fate worse than death, if you like."

"I don't like!" Putnam said firmly. "Your job is to find Anthony Bowdler Cromwell. So far you've managed to get involved in two murders, one assault, and an attempted rape. And I don't see that you're any closer to locating Cromwell than you were three days ago. Just what have you accomplished, Mr. Victor?"

"I've woo'd and won the lady of my double's choice."

"I beg your pardon?"

"I'm engaged to be married."

"Congratulations. But you can't let your personal life interfere with this case. It's too important. If it's going to get in the way, perhaps you should postpone the nuptials."

"Can I quote you on that?"

"Of course not. As far as your bride-to-be is concerned,

I don't even exist. I hope you haven't told her about what you're working on. Women are prone to talk. And that would be a decided breach of security."

"Don't worry, I haven't. Anyway, she's much too busy making plans for the wedding to worry about a little thing like national security."

"Good. Let her go on worrying about the wedding. That should leave you free to wrap up this Cromwell business."

"I'll do my best."

"Please try to do better. So far your best seems slated to earn you the dubious distinction of being Public Enemy Number One."

With that remark, delivered in a quietly scathing tone, Putnam hailed a cab and left me. He'd done his job—secured my release from the police once again—and I guess he figured there wasn't much else he could do, so he might as well leave me on my own and hope for the best. I hoped along with him as I continued up the street alone, wondering if I should make another stab at seeing Ingrid, or if I should head back to my hotel. Finally, disgusted and tired, I decided on the hotel.

The night clerk had eighteen messages for me when I came through the lobby. Fifteen of them were from Hortense, asking me to call her back as soon as I came in. The other three were from Ingrid, Elsa and Gretchen respectively. Gretchen? It took me a minute to place her. Ahh, yes, she was the spank-party lassie my impersonator had made such an impression on. What could she want? For that matter, what did Elsa want? Or Ingrid?

"Lots of excitement over the wedding, I guess." The night clerk smiled at me.

"Oodles," I agreed drily.

"The manager was wondering if you've considered holding it in the hotel. I hope you don't mind my mentioning it, Mr. Victor."

114

"Not at all. No, I haven't thought about holding it in the hotel. The truth is I haven't thought about it at all. I prefer it that way."

"I know how it is," the clerk said in a soothing tone. "I'm married myself."

"Are you now?"

"Yes, sir. And how well I remember what it was like. All the confusion and everything. Weddings are really for the ladies, don't you think, sir?"

"Weddings," I told him firmly, "are strictly for the birds."

My vehemence surprised him. I left him mulling it over and went up to my room. I put the message from Hortense to one side. Eeny-meeny-miny-mo—Ingrid came up first. I recognized the number she'd left. It was Helen Quentin's.

"Hello." I returned her greeting. "Steve Victor here. Is Ingrid there?"

"Yes, she is. But before you talk to her, there are a few things I have to say to you. Murdering George was one thing, but this business tonight with Patricia is something else again. That was simply unforgiveable!"

"The quality of mercy—"

"Has been strained too far!" she finished for me indignantly. "Even our little group has its rules, Mr. Victor. And one of them is that we don't assault children. I haven't spoken to the rest of the members, but in view of your actions, I'm sure they'll agree with me that you're not our sort of person!"

Well, it isn't everybody who gets drummed out of a wife-swapping club. I guessed it was a distinction of a sort. "Look," I told her, "you can tear off my epaulets and strip me of my rank the next time I see you. But for now, how about letting me speak to Ingrid?"

"Very well. I just wanted you to know how I feel. I never like to blackball anybody anonymously."

"I'm overwhelmed by your ethics. Now how about Ingrid?"

"Here she is."

"Hello." Ingrid's deep-throated voice was as blonde and bosomy as she was.

"I have to talk to you about Knute Hajstrom," I told her.

"Talk? After you killed him!"

"Who did he kill now?" I heard Helen Quentin inquire in the background.

"Nobody you know, dear," Ingrid assured her hastily.

"You don't want to talk over the phone with Helen there," I guessed. "When can we get together?"

"I don't think I should get together with you. You're a very dangerous man. You might decide to kill me."

"Now why would I want to do that?"

"I don't know. Why did you want to kill Knute?"

"I didn't. And I didn't kill him."

"I saw you. Remember?"

"Who's Knute?" Helen asked.

"Nobody important. Honestly, darling—"

"You're lying!" Helen said. "I can always tell! So help me, Ingrid, if you've been—"

"I haven't," Ingrid lied. "Really I haven't! Just look at all the trouble you're causing," she said into the mouthpiece.

"Then get yourself up here where we can talk alone." I decided to play it hard. "If you don't, I'll tell Helen all about you and Hajstrom. And maybe I'll tell Phil about your being with Helen tonight, too."

"But I can't. I don't have the car. Phil's using it."

"Take a cab!" I told her. "I'll be waiting." On that note I hung up, reasonably sure she'd come over.

Elsa was next. I dialed the number she'd left. Barry answered. His voice was sleepy. "She's sound asleep," his voice yawned in my ear. "Can't imagine what she

116

wanted. Probably something about the arrangements for getting together tomorrow night. I'll leave her a note to call you in the morning."

I thanked him and hung up. That left the mysterious Gretchen. Never having met the lady, I had no idea what to say to her. I decided to play it by ear.

"Mr. Victor. I have information for you," she said when I identified myself. "It is urgent that I see you immediately."

"Immediately, I'm a little bit tied up," I told her. "Can't it wait until tomorrow?"

"I can wait. But can you? From the way you spoke last night, I gathered that you were in a hurry—about Carrie Cromwell, I mean. Perhaps I was wrong."

"You weren't wrong," I told her. "What about Carrie Cromwell?"

"You meant what you said about the money?"

"Absolutely," I assured her, not having the slightest idea what she was talking about.

"But it should be more now."

"Oh? Why?"

"Because of last night. You didn't tell me you were going to kill the Swede. If I had known that, I wouldn't have agreed to take you there. Now it is more dangerous, and I should have more money."

"We'll talk about it when I see you," I suggested.

"Can I come to your hotel tonight?"

"Give me about three hours," I told her, figuring that I'd be through with Ingrid by then.

"All right. Goodbye until then." Gretchen hung up.

I'd no sooner put the receiver back in the cradle than the phone rang again. It was Elsa. Her voice was a muffled whisper.

"Barry's asleep again," she said. "I don't want to take a chance on waking him. I couldn't get the phone fast enough before, so I pretended to be asleep. I couldn't let him hear us talking. I have something important to tell you. I'm going to sneak out now and take the car. I should be at your hotel in half an hour."

"Hey, wait a mi—" I started to say. It was too late. Elsa had hung up.

No rest for the weary. I decided that what I needed was a hot shower and a change of clothes to get rid of the traces of my adventures with Patricia. I was just buttoning myself into a clean shirt when the phone rang again. It was Elsa, calling from the lobby.

"Come on up," I told her.

"I think it's better if I speak to you alone," she said.

"I'm alone."

"You are? But what about your wife? Isn't she with you?"

Wife? I remembered then that Elsa thought Hortense and I were a married couple. "She's away for the evening, visiting her mother," I improvised. "So come on up to the room. It's safe."

A few minutes later I answered her knock at the door and she came inside. "Barry would be angry enough to kill us both if he knew I'd come to you," she announced breathlessly in that birdlike peep-peep voice of hers.

"If he wants to kill me, he'll just have to wait his turn," I informed her. "There may be a husband or two and sundry other guys in line before him."

"I'll just bet there are!" She looked at me archly, her hand fluttering at the bodice of the low-cut dress she'd put on, an oriole preening its plumage. "Aren't you going to offer me a drink?" she wanted to know.

"Sure." I slopped some Scotch into a glass and handed it to her. "But you didn't come all this way just for a drink," I reminded her.

"I might have. If I'd been asked, that is."

"I'm flattered. But I'm also a little short on time. You'd be doing me a favor if you'd come to the point."

She turned into a pouter pigeon. "I don't think you really like me at all," she brooded.

"I'm wild about you." I made my voice sound sincere.

"Do you mean that, Steve? Gosh, I hope so. Because ever since the other night, I've had a real thing for you. I don't know why, but you really get to me. I felt it last night, too. Otherwise I wouldn't have done what you asked."

What had I asked? "But you did do it," I prompted her. "And how did it turn out?"

"Oh!" She rolled her somewhat beady bird-eyes. "Barry would just kill me if he knew!"

"Why? Why should Barry be jealous? From what I've seen he seems to take a pretty liberal attitude toward—"

"He wouldn't be jealous," she interrupted, chirping with laughter at the idea. "He'd be mad because I pried into his affairs. With the Cromwell woman, I mean."

"Oh. I see. And what did you find out?"

"You can ask nicer than that." She pursed her lips like a sparrow going after an earthworm.

I kissed her, and she clung to me. "Now tell me about the Cromwell woman," I crooned into her ear.

"Barry took her to a spank-party at Von Koerner's while I was out of town," she chirruped, taking my hand between hers and inserting it in her loose bodice.

"I already found that out," I said.

"Oh? How? Well, never mind. I found out something else that's sure to interest you." Elsa nuzzled her bare breast against the palm of my hand so that the tip embedded itself between two of my fingers. "Do you think I'm too small?" she asked.

"What?"

"My breasts? Are they too small? You see, I've always had this inferiority complex, and I'm so anxious to please you—"

"They're fine. Just perfect. Now what about Carrie Cromwell?"

"I sneaked the key from Barry's desk out of his pocket and went through the drawers. I found a slip of paper with her address and phone number on it." Elsa's hand dropped to my thigh and trailed upward. "I know where she is," she tweeted.

"Where?"

"You'd never guess in a million years." Her hand slid under the waistband of my pants and grabbed.

"I won't even try to guess. You're going to tell me, aren't you, honey?" I made my voice as intimate as her caress was.

"Ooh! I go all shivery when you call me honey that way. Say it again." Her hand tightened.

"Ouch! Honey."

"Sorry. I got carried away, I guess. Let me kiss it and make it better."

"In a minute. First tell me where Carrie Cromwell is."

"No, first I want to—"

There was a sudden knock at the door, and her head shot up even faster than it had been lowered.

"Mr. Victor?" a voice called out.

"That's Ingrid!" Elsa hissed. "What's she doing here? She mustn't find me! It would be just like her to tell Barry."

"Just a minute," I called back. "I'm not dressed. I'm sorry, but I just stepped out of the shower. I don't have a stitch on. Why don't you wait for me down in the lobby? It's more comfortable than standing there. I'll come down and get you just as soon as I throw something on."

"Oh, all right." Ingrid sounded annoyed.

"You think fast," Elsa said admiringly, her head sinking to its former position again.

"Sorry, baby, but we don't have time." I pulled her firmly to her feet. "Now suppose you tell me where Carrie Cromwell is, and I'll get you out of here before Ingrid comes back and spots you."

"Damn! I suppose you're right. Well, brace yourself. Carrie Cromwell is right here in this very hotel. She's registered here with her husband. That was the address and phone number I found in Barry's desk. And she's still registered here. I checked with the desk clerk. Now, aren't you proud of me?"

"You've been a big help," I lied. I saw no reason to tell her that the Cromwells were still registered because Putnam had seen to it so that their disappearance wouldn't cause any more of a stir than it already had. "Do you have anything else to tell me?"

"Just that she called Barry tonight. I eavesdropped. She wanted to make sure he was coming to Von Koerner's tomorrow. And from the conversation, I gathered that she wanted to be sure he was bringing you. What gives with you and her, anyway? Why can't you contact each other directly? Does it have something to do with O. R. G. Y.? Is she working for you?"

"No time for questions," I told her, steering her into the hall. "Now you wait around this bend here until you see me come up with Ingrid. Then you can go down to the lobby and get out without her spotting you." I gave her a quick kiss goodbye and started for the lobby myself.

"Ooh, Steve, wait!" Elsa called after me. "I forgot to tell you something else."

"What?"

"That Gretchen called me earlier this evening. You know, the fat-chested blonde."

"Yeah. I know her. What did she want?"

"Your phone number. She said she had to reach you.

121

She said you split in such a hurry last night that you didn't have a chance to exchange numbers. I didn't know you saw her after you left us. I'll bet your wife doesn't know, either. You are a naughty boy. I could be very jealous about that, you know."

"Elsa, you're the only woman for me. Outside of my wife, of course," I reminded myself.

"Anyway, I gave her the number. The flabby-bosomed wench, I mean. But even so, that doesn't mean you have to start up with her."

"I won't," I assured her. "I'm spoken for." I blew Elsa a kiss as the elevator doors opened, stepped inside, and pushed the button for the lobby. Well, anyway, now I knew how come Gretchen had contacted me instead of my Russian double. And that was really about all that Elsa had told me that was helpful.

The look on Ingrid's face when I strolled across the lobby toward her didn't promise that she was planning to be too helpful, either. The look said she wasn't used to being kept waiting. With her charms, there was no reason why she should have been used to it. Scenery-wise, Ingrid was a decided improvement over Elsa. When it came to conversation, though, the eye-filling blonde was nowhere. She didn't say a word all the way up to the room. And the glare she shot me when I closed the door behind us was decidedly hostile.

"Would you like a drink?" I asked her.

"No. What do you want?" Her tone was arrogant, but there was a hint of fear in the way she kept her distance from me.

"Relax. I'm not going to bite you."

"I wouldn't be here at all if you hadn't blackmailed me into coming."

"All right then. I'll come to the point. I want you to tell me everything you know about Knute Hajstrom."

"You mean your victim! One of them, anyway!"

"If you like." I was getting tired of denying my murderous nature. "When did you meet him? How?"

"Velvet arranged it."

"Did he, now!" That was something to think about. "How come?"

"The same reason he arranged for you to go to the Quentins. Money. Hajstrom paid him."

"But how come Velvet steered him to you?"

"Hajstrom wasn't just looking for some underground fun. He was looking for a woman."

"Carrie Cromwell," I guessed.

"Yes. But I didn't know that at the time. The way I figure it, he paid Velvet through the nose to get a lead on Carrie. But even so, Velvet was afraid to give him a direct lead. He didn't know what might be involved, but he was scared. Too scared to steer Hajstrom directly to Barry, who knew Carrie Cromwell. Or even to the Quentins, where she'd gone with Barry one night. So Velvet just sort of steered him to me, which was a sort of indirect lead in a way."

"Do you know where Carrie Cromwell is?"

"No. That's what Hajstrom kept trying to find out from me. But I'd only met her the one time. All I knew was that Barry knew her."

"Did you tell Hajstrom that?"

"No. I just told him I might know someone who could help him."

"Why didn't you level with him?"

"I was teasing him along. It kept him coming back for more."

"Coming back to the 'Friends of Sweden,' you mean?"

"Yes."

"But why were you leading him down the garden path that way?" I wondered.

"Because I knew that once I told him what he wanted to know, I'd probably never see him again."

"Were you in love with Hajstrom?"

"Not exactly. Not the way you mean, anyway. It was his eyes." Her own eyes shone as she said it.

"His eyes?"

"Yes. The way he looked at me when I used to strip for the camera bugs at 'Friends of Sweden.' It flipped me, that look of his. Sometimes I'd take him off into a room where we could be alone and just dance for him naked while he watched. His eyes on my body drove me nuts. I could really make it that way, just watching him ogling my naked body. His eyes were like the eyes of an animal: savage, filled with lust, but deep and mysterious, too. Sometimes I could catch the reflection of my naked flesh in their depths, and then I'd really go over the top."

"Is that the only way you could make it?"

"Yes." She looked at me defiantly.

"Just with Hajstrom?" I asked curiously. "Or with other voyeur types as well?"

"Oh, I could do it with others. That's why I started going there in the first place. But it was best with Knute."

"Is that what you were doing the night he was killed?"

"That's what we were about to do. But I had to go—umm—powder my nose, if you know what I mean."

"I know what you mean. So you weren't actually there when he was killed."

"If you mean when you stuck that sword into him, no. But you still had it in your hand with the blood dripping from it when I came back. Remember?"

"That I remember," I granted her. "Do you have any idea why he was killed?"

"That's one hell of a question for you to be asking me!"

"Take a stab at it anyway," I prodded her.

"Something to do with Carrie Cromwell, I guess. You

were both looking for her. What makes that dame so important?"

"Her husband," I said truthfully. "Did you ever run across him in your travels?"

"I didn't even know she had one," Ingrid said. "And if you're through asking questions, can I go now?"

"Yes. You can go. Mine eyes have seen the glory—and once is enough!"

That riled her, as I'd known it would. "I didn't notice you pulling down your lids the other night," she said indignantly.

"Different circumstances."

"What do you mean?"

"Then I could sample the texture. Now it's a case of look, but don't touch. I don't get my kicks that way."

"If you weren't so nasty—and so murderous—"

"Thanks all the same, but this is one of my busy nights."

"It's your loss."

"Is it?"

Ingrid was facing the door now, away from me. She stood there for a full minute and suddenly whirled about. She'd unbuttoned her dress all the way down the front. She wasn't wearing anything underneath it. Her hands were under her breasts, thrusting them towards me like some sort of sacrificial offering. The lower part of her body was moving in slow circles, the hips rotating, the belly undulating, the triangle of blonde curls pulsating over pink, quivering nether lips.

I'm human. I gasped. I stared.

The stare—that was all she wanted. Her hand dropped down, and a few seconds later a spasm shook her whole body. It was more than pleasure for her. It was an insult flung in my face.

"Yes," she said. "It is your loss." Her hands flew up

125

the buttons of her dress, and then she was going out the door.

"Give my regards to Phil," I called after her. "Or Helen, as the case may be."

I crossed over and closed the door behind her. Then I looked at my watch. There was still an hour to go before Gretchen was due. I curled up on the bed and grabbed a little snooze.

The phone woke me. It was the downstairs desk. Gretchen was there. I told them to send her up. I threw some cold water on my face and was just finishing combing my hair when she knocked.

I opened the door on a woman-and-a-half in a one-woman bag. Not that there was anything baggy about the dress Gretchen was wearing. Far from it. Her curves hugged the red silk so tightly that I figured the only way she could have gotten into it was by having someone blow her up into it like a balloon. Then I figured again—There was so much to Gretchen that I had to blink for a second look before I could take it all in. She was six feet tall—maybe an inch or so over—and with the heels she was wearing, she towered over me by a good two inches. I'd say she weighed about 150 to 160 pounds. But don't get the wrong idea. There wasn't an inch of fat on her. About half her weight was in three spots—her bosom, her hips, and her *derriere*. Yes, I guess the last-mentioned was a trifle plump, but it was firm and high and a natural focal point for any male eye.

She was the kind of woman all men admire, but are not necessarily attracted to. There was so much of her that many a man might be intimidated by all that pulchritude. Women, it follows, would resent her on sight. Gretchen would make almost all females feel inadequate. I hoped for my sake that my double leaned more toward sadism than masochism. The very idea of playing victim to this Amazon—even by proxy—gave me butterflies in the tum-tum. I was scared she might want to pick up where my Russian look-alike had left off. On the other hand, if it was the other way around, Gretchen was an awful lot of territory to cover—even with a whip.

She wore her long blonde hair loose and straight to the waist. The only makeup she had on was lipstick. She didn't need anything else. Her eyes out-blued any mascara I'd ever seen, and her cheeks were red as ripe tomatoes with a touch of fever. They were even redder than the dress, which had a deep V neckline which followed her naturally deep cleavage. On either side of the V, the dress pushed straight out an impossible distance. Her breasts were so mammoth, you'd figure they'd have to be pulled downward by their own weight. But they weren't. They stuck out firmly with no trace of sag, a mammarian defiance of the law of gravity.

"My goodness," Gretchen said, "you'd think you'd never seen me before. Do I look that much better in clothes?"

"Sorry." I remembered my manners and mixed her a drink. I mixed one for myself as well. I needed it. "You said you had some information about Carrie Cromwell," I reminded her as she took a sip.

"And you said we'd discuss the matter of money. Five thousand isn't enough."

"Isn't it? Why not?"

"You killed the Swede. You might decide to kill Carrie Cromwell. If you got caught, I might be implicated. The risk is worth more than five thousand."

"Why should I kill Carrie Cromwell?"

"Why did you kill the Swede?"

She had me there. Why *had* Stevkovsky killed the Swede?

"When you wangled me into taking you there," Gretchen continued, "you never said anything about murder. That wasn't in the deal."

"Maybe you'd better refresh my memory about the deal," I suggested.

"Well," she admitted, "I guess it wasn't exactly a deal. You just said something kiddingly about how this O. R. G. Y. outfit of yours was going to catch up with the times and do a survey of sex in outer space. And I told you about this fellow Hajstrom who might be just the one for you to talk to because he was some kind of space scientist from Sweden and a swinger besides. You wanted to know what I meant by a swinger, so I told you about 'Friends of Sweden,' and how the first time I went there was because I was a model and this Swedish photographer friend of mine took me there. I said it was a gas, and you said how you'd like to go there and maybe meet this scientist. So we arranged to meet after you ditched your wife, and I took you up there and introduced you to Hajstrom. I never should have left you alone with him. I never figured to be fingering him so you could kill him. But I'm not going to make the same mistake about Carrie Cromwell. If you want to know where she is to kill her, the price has gone up to ten grand."

"It might be worth it," I fenced with Gretchen, "if I had some assurance that her husband was with her."

"Husband? I didn't even know she had one." Gretchen got to her feet. "Well, take it or leave it," she aaid firmly.

"I think that Mr. Victor will leave it."

Fear stamped itself on Gretchen's face as she stared at the doorway from which the voice had spoken. I whirled around to look at the intruder. I had no trouble identifying him immediately. Bald, a scar on his cheek, monocle —it all matched Hortense's description of Von Koerner.

"What are you doing here?" I couldn't think of anything else to say.

"One of my—ahh—servants overheard Gretchen speaking to you on the telephone," he informed us as he closed the door firmly behind him. "I feared that she might be interfering with my plans for negotiating with you. Now, from what I have just heard, I see that my fears were well founded. You have been very naughty and disloyal, Gretchen. I shall really have to discipline you."

He was carrying a sleek black walking stick with a silver knob. Now he riased it so that it was parallel with his hip. A split second later, a sharp blade, about three inches long, sprang from its tip.

"Yes, you must learn your lesson, Gretchen." The cane was a quick blur slashing at her body with two quick strokes. The red resss parted horizontally at the very tips of her bosom. Blood, a darker red, immediately covered the exposed portion of her flesh. "Now do you see why you must remain loyal, Gretchen?" Von Koerner asked in a calm voice.

It happened so fast that she didn't even scream. She just moaned her anguish as she sank to her knees, her hands clutching at herself to stem the bleeding. Between her fingertips, I could see that he had neatly pierced the tips of both breasts. But, like Gretchen, I was so stunned by the suddenness of it that it was a moment before I reacted.

Then I did react. I was outraged, and I moved unthinkingly. "You dirty—!" I dived for Von Koerner.

He took one step to the side, and the cane flashed out again. I braked to a halt with the blade nicking at my throat. It stayed there, pricking me as I backed away. Finally it forced me to sit down in a chair. Then it still hovered a scant quarter inch from my jugular.

"Now answer the phone, Mr. Victor."

It must have been ringing for a while. I hadn't heard

it. I'd been too busy trying to keep my head on my shoulders. Now, automatically, I reached for it.

"Act natural. Be very careful what you say," Von Koerner instructed, twirling the blade a little to drive home his point.

I gulpèd and nodded to show I understood. I picked up the phone. "Hello."

"Hello, Steve, darling?" It was Hortense. "I know it's awful of me to call you in the middle of the night like this, but I just had to tell you."

"Tell me what?" I was getting cross-eyed from focussing on the blade's tip.

"About our wedding. You'll never guess who I've persuaded to give me away."

"Give you away?" My voice squeaked. Von Koerner didn't want it to squeak. The blade scratched me slightly. I cleared my throat.

"I mean give away the bride, silly." Hortense sounded very bubbly. "Guess who's going to do it?"

"Who?"

"None other than Senator Alvin K. Leander himself. What do you think of that?"

"Fine. That's fine." Von Koerner was getting impatient. I tried to suck in my throat.

"It wasn't easy to get him to agree, but I reminded him of a few things, and asked very sweetly after his wife, and he said he'd be delighted. He was really very chivalrous about it."

"That's nice."

"Well, you could be more enthusiastic. I did it for you, darling. I want you to be proud of your bride."

"I'm very proud." Von Koerner's impatience had him on the verge of performing a tracheotomy.

"I knew you would be. And, Steve, darling, I wanted to ask you about your mother. I respect her religious convictions. I want you to know that. But don't you think with the Senator coming and all she might be a little tolerant. It's bound to look funny if she isn't there. I thought maybe if I called her—"

"End it!" Von Koerner hissed. The blade drew blood.

"You do that," I told Hortense. "Let me know how you make out."

"Wait! Don't hang up yet, darling!" she said.

"Hang up!" Von Koerner insisted.

"You'd better do as he says," Gretchen moaned. "He'd think nothing of killing you."

"Steve! What's that voice? Do you have a woman in your room?"

"I won't. I will. Yes. No," I answered confusedly.

"Steve! Another woman! With the wedding only a few days off! How could you?"

"Just lucky, I guess," I said weakly.

"Steve!"

"Hang up!"

"He'll kill you!"

The voices assailed me. The blade pierced my flesh, hungry for my blood. Crazily, a bizarre solution to all my troubles flashed across my mind. I'd ask Von Koerner to be my best man! And Gretchen could be a bridesmaid!

chapter
NINE

"Look," I told Hortense. "There's no woman here. I just left the radio on. That's all. And I'm awfully sleepy right now. Can't we talk about the wedding arrangements in the morning, my pet?"

"Look," I hissed at Gretchen. "Just shut up, will you?"

"Look," I pleaded with Von Koerner. "If you'll stop trying to skewer my Adam's apple, I'll get off the phone right away."

"All right," Hortense agreed.

"All right," Gretchen agreed.

"All right," Von Koerner agreed—and released the pressure on the blade at my throat.

Hortense hung up—finally. Gretchen cowered in a corner. Von Koerner smiled a humorless smile and kept the cane poised. "And now to business, Mr. Victor. It was really very foolish of you to bother with Gretchen here," he told me. "She isn't even aware of the existence of the one you really seek. She would have arranged for you to meet Carrie Cromwell, but you would have thrown your money away. In the first place, I had already made arrangements for you to meet her free of charge."

"Then it was you who had her call Barry tonight to make sure I'd come tomorrow evening," I guessed.

"Correct. So you see, you should thank me. I have saved you ten thousand dollars. Or was it only five? No matter. In any case it would have been a dead end for you. It isn't Carrie Cromwell you want. It's her husband. I know that. And only I am in a position to help you."

"Do you have Anthony Bowdler Cromwell?"

"I can produce him. For a price, naturally."

"What price?"

"One hundred thousand dollars."

"She only wanted ten thousand." I jerked my thumb at Gretchen.

"For the wife, yes. But I have the genuine article. And, I might add, if you aren't interested, there are others who are."

"What others?"

"Hajstrom was one."

"He's dead," I reminded Von Koerner.

"Yes. Most unfortunate. I really don't know what you hoped to accomplish by that. I'm sure his people will arrange to contact me despite his unfortunate demise."

I got a glimmering of why Stevkovsky had killed Hajstrom. Sure! The piece fit neatly into place. Von Koerner was offering Cromwell to the highest bidder. And Stevkovsky had simply eliminated Hajstrom to cut down the chances of being outbid.

"Who else is in the running?" I asked Von Koerner.

"The Russians. The Chinese. The Egyptians. Many countries have reason to want Cromwell's process."

"Do you have the process?"

"No. But I can produce Cromwell. After that, it's up to you. Of course, I'm assuming that you're in a position to speak for your government. If you are, I'm sure they'll see the logic of meeting my price."

"Suppose that instead we just lock you up for the

treacherous kidnapping blackmailer you are and throw away the key?"

"That would not be wise. Believe me. Cromwell would never be seen again. Arrangements have been made to cover such an eventuality. If anything happens to me, Cromwell's fate is sealed."

"You certainly have a way with words," I told him sarcastically. "But before I advise my government to fork over a hundred grand, I have to be awfully damn sure that they'll get what they're paying for."

"That can be arranged," Von Koerner assured me. "Do you think you can have the money for me—in small, unmarked bills, of course—when you come to our little discipline meeting tomorrow night?"

"If I've gotten the reassurance I require."

"Very well." Von Koerner handed me a card. "Come to this address at two tomorrow afternoon and you shall have it. Ask for me. Then we can conclude our business when we meet later on in the evening." Von Koerner grabbed Gretchen by her elbow and pulled her to her feet. Still holding his cane at the ready, he propelled her to the door. "Good night, Mr. Victor." He flicked his thumb, and the blade snapped back into the walking stick. The door closed behind them.

I hit the sack. But I couldn't fall asleep. There was too much to think about. There were still too many unanswered questions. There was the card Von Koerner had given me for instance: Embossed letter spelling out "RESEARCH INSTITUTE OF ADVANCED GYNECOLOGY," an address beneath, and in the lower right hand corner Von Koerner's name with a "Dr." in front of it. What sort of place was it? I wondered. What was Von Koerner's position there? What did it have to do with Anthony Bowdler Cromwell? Was that where he was being held? I doubted it. Von Koerner wouldn't take that kind of chance. But then how would my going there provide me with proof that Von Koerner could really produce Cromwell?

Other questions—disconnected ones—also chased themselves around my head. How had Hajstrom come to Von Koerner? Gretchen had seemed unaware of any connection between them. And what about Carrie Cromwell? How had she gotten involved with Von Koerner? Had she delivered her husband into his clutches? Knowingly? If so, why? And how had Von Koerner known of Cromwell's importance in the first place? Also, what of Stevkovsky? How had he gotten onto Cromwell's invention? Had Von Koerner approached the Russians? If so, why had my double had to follow my trail and impersonate me in order to get to von Koerner?

Most intriguing of all, who was Von Koerner, anyway? Who did he represent? A gang? Some secret organization? An international outfit loyal only to itself and ready to sell to any side for its own profit? Or was Von Koerner strictly a loner engaged in a onetime venture he'd stumbled into, a loner operating probably with the help of a few hired thugs?

Questions! Questions! Questions!

I fell asleep.

The phone—trustier than any alarm clock—woke me as usual. It was Hortense—as usual. Her voice was starry-eyed with wedding plans—as usual.

"Steve, I'd like your opinion about the caterer. Now, he advised . . ."

I tuned out. I looked at my wristwatch lying on the night-table. It was almost noon. And I was due at the Research Institute at two o'clock.

"Yeah, honey." I interrupted Hortense in mid-sentence. "That sounds dandy. We can go over the details when I see you tonight." I hung up before she could object.

Next I dialed Putnam. "American original," I identified myself. "I need a hundred thousand dollars in small, unmarked bills."

"You must be planning a pretty big wedding."

"It's for your boy with the mousetrap. That's the asking price."

"How sure are you that the people you're dealing with can deliver?"

"I'm not sure. But I should know one way or the other by tonight. Can you get the money up to my hotel about seven?"

"The government doesn't like to pay ransom," Putnam told me.

"I'm a taxpayer. Neither do I. And maybe we can get it back in the long run. But the first thing is to get the mousetrap builder back safe, isn't it?"

"Yes. You're right. We can't afford to take chances. I'll see that you get the money." Putnam hung up.

I got dressed, ate a huge brunch, and headed for the Research Institute. It was five of two when I got there. I stood in front of it for a moment, looking the place over.

Only four stories, but impressive. Clean lines, glass front, sterile steel. Very modern. Very utilitarian. Very impressive!

Two pyramids with a phallic sweep to them flanked the front entrance outside. I walked between them. Inside a pair of wire mobiles pointed an aisle toward a center reception desk. The desk was marble. I walked up to it.

"I'd like to see Dr. Von Koerner," I told the pleasantly smiling middle-aged woman behind it.

"Do you have an appointment?"

"Yes. He's expecting me."

Her fingers went tic-tac-toe over the switchboard at her side, and she leaned discreetly into the echo-proof mouthpiece. Then she leaned back toward me and showed me some more of her dentures.

"Room three-one-six, third floor. The elevator's right over there." She nodded in the direction she meant.

The elevator was automatic and over-pressurized. It made my ears pop. They popped back as I entered room three-one-six.

"Mr. Victor?" More teeth from the girl behind the desk. She was younger. I guessed they were her own.

"Yes, I admitted.

"You can go right in. Doctor is waiting for you." She indicated a door to her right.

I went through it. Doctor was indeed waiting for me. His smile of greeting was even less sincere than the other two. "Mr. Victor. I'm so glad you came."

For a hundred thousand dollars, I bet he was glad. "*Doctor* Von Koerner?" I made it a question more than a greeting.

"Oh, yes," he acknowledged it. "I am indeed a doctor, Mr. Victor."

"A doctor of what?" I asked curiously.

"Gynecology. I do not like to brag, but at one time I was one of the best-known gynecologists in Berlin."

"West Berlin, or East Berlin?" It was a dig.

He recognized it as such and raised an eyebrow. "I went wherever my practice took me, Mr. Victor."

"And always ended up in the same old place."

"Of course." He gave me a cold smile. "But then I am forgetting that our professions are closely related, aren't I? We are, in a sense, colleagues."

"Oh, I wouldn't say that. We're only loosely in the same field. Gynecology is only of the most casual concern to O. R. G. Y."

"But my interests extend far beyond the field of gynecology." Von Koerner waved an arm. "This Institute, of

137

which I am the director, has followed its nose—I beg your pardon; an unfortunate choice of words—has extended itself, rather, in directions which are not dissimilar to those pursued by O. R. G. Y. Currently we are engaged in a series of experiments and observations designed to provide data relating to psychological and physical reactions of people engaging in the sex act."

"You mean you've been surveying people as to their reactions?"

"Not at all. What we have been doing is actually observing and taking measurements while the act of intercourse is performed."

"You mean going into the bedrooms of married couples and—?"

"No. The people come here. To the Institute. Volunteers. And while we began with married couples, today we by no means limit ourselves to them. Many single people of both sexes come here. Some of them are paid. We use both male and female prostitutes. But many other single people simply come in the interests of abetting scientific investigation—or perhaps merely to satisfy their desire. It is fascinating work. I am truly saddened that I shall have to give it up."

"It sounds fascinating. But why do you have to give it up?"

"Oh, come now, Mr. Victor. You don't imagine that once we have concluded our business dealings I would be so foolish as to remain within catching distance. If you have entertained any such notion, let me assure you that foolproof arrangements have been made for me to disappear as soon as the matter is concluded. If that weren't so, I should never have invited you here."

"Just why did you ask me here? I thought it was to provide proof that you could produce Cromwell."

"So it is. And you shall have your proof. If you will be so good as to come with me." Von Koerner held the

138

door open and then guided me down the hallway. We went into another room, an antechamber of some sort, and then through another door.

Now we were in a very large and very unusual room. The center area was taken up by a sort of bedroom setup. It was pleasant, not exactly plush, but well-appointed in the modern fashion. The furnishings were in good taste, yet there were voluptuous touches not found in the ordinary boudoir.

The double bed was king-size, covered with a positively lascivious red spread, and there must have been eight or ten pillows of different colors strewn suggestively atop it. There was a vanity, mirrored and neat, but with a variety of bottles of scent on it that would have been worthy of a Turkish harem. A wardrobe closet, sturdy and sensible, stood with its sliding doors opened. Inside I could see a variety of female lingerie and men's sleepwear. There were styles and patterns to suit every taste with the stress on erotic appeal. Across from it was a make-believe window with drapes and a venetian blind.

Von Koerner turned out the light on the nightstand beside the bed and then raised the blinds. There was a flat on the other side of it with a very clever simulation of an evening sky. Von Kvoerner pushed a few buttons, and a moon and a spattering of stars lit up most realistically. He turned them out again and turned on the lights.

Now we proceeded to the outer section of the large chamber. The "bedroom" took up the center area, but the scene beyond its fringes was completely different. Here, ringing it, was the most elaborate sort of laboratory equipment. There were machines and electrographs and recording instruments and banks of levers and a variety of other gadgets, most of which were meaningless to me. Von Koerner undertook to explain their functions.

"Do you see that mirror?' He pointed. I hadn't noticed it before, but the ceiling suspended over the "bedroom"

139

was all mirrored glass. "It serves several functions," Von Koerner continued. "It provides erotic encouragement; that, of course, is obvious. It also serves as a one-way viewing glass by which we can watch our subjects while they engage in sex. And there are a series of motion-picture cameras which photograph them from every angle in full color. Built into the furniture of the room are tape recorders which pick up the slightest sound, right down to variations in the sonics of the subjects' breathing. In the springs of the mattress itself are tiny transistor devices which connect up to this electro-cardiogram machine here and record the subjects' pulse beats." He indicated the machine of which he spoke.

"How do you tell their heart beats apart?" I asked.

"Each heart has its own individual pattern. The differences are minute, but detectable. By ferreting them out beforehand, we are able to distinguish one from the other in the graphs recorded by the machine."

"I see."

"Also, electrical connections from much of the apparatus are directly made to the subjects themselves. This machine records their brain waves as transmitted by electrodes fastened to their temples. This one measures both the extent and chemical content of their perspiration. Special vents in the experimental area pick up odors and transmit them to this machine which records their intensity and individualistic nature. All of these things tell us much about the subjects' psychological reactions, as well as their physical ones. Perspiration may be a sign of fear, for instance. What was it that the subject found threatening at that particular moment? By correlating our data, we can determine that—as well as many other things."

"How do you correlate?"

"Do you see that large computer over there with the bank of switches and flashing lights?"

"Yes. I was going to ask what it was."

140

"We call it the 'Brain.' All the information compiled by these other devices is fed directly into it. The 'Brain' has ten thousand cross-circuits of categorization. Therefore, the punch card it eventually releases on each individual subject is the result of a truly infinite number of possible combinations. Its calculations are so complex as to be well beyond the scope of the human mind. Therefore, when it reports similarities among subjects, we must accept such similarities as a pattern of human behavior. If twenty people have identical physical or psychological reactions during the sex act, the mathematical odds are too enormously against it being mere coincidence for that to be a consideration. Do you follow, Mr. Victor? It's not a question of twenty to one. Because of the infinite number of patterns the 'Brain' is capable of detecting, it is a matter of billions and billions to one. Such evidence must be accepted."

"I'm not questioning it. What I do question is the value of reducing human sexual behavior to the confines of a pigeonhole."

"But isn't that exactly what O. R. G. Y. does? The only difference, if you'll pardon me, is that our methods are more efficient."

"And a damn sight less fun," I pointed out.

"Perhaps. But then you shall have the opportunity of determining that for yourself. If you have no objection, Mr. Victor, I shall ask you to participate in one of our experiments."

"And if I have some objection? I'm sure it would be very interesting, but that isn't what I came here for."

"That's where you're wrong, Mr. Victor. That's exactly why I had you come here. Believe me, it will provide the assurance you seek regarding our impending transaction."

I wouldn't have believed Von Koerner if he'd been perched on the proverbial stack of Bibles. But I had no choice except to go along with what he wanted. It was his show, and he was calling the shots. I had to play his game if I wanted to find Cromwell. My only consolation was the fact that it wouldn't be to his advantage to harm me. I was the in-between slated to make the payoff. Because of this, Von Koerner would have been willing to take out a Blue Shield policy on me if that might have kept me healthy. So I shrugged and agreed to go along with his cockamamie program.

"Good. Then I shall leave you now. I suggest that you prepare for bed. Help yourself to anything that appeals to you." He gestured toward the wardrobe closet. "Just relax and enjoy yourself," Von Koerner advised politely, and then he left.

Feeling like a guppie in a goldfish bowl, I strode over to the wardrobe. I selected some black silk pajamas; they were conservative compared to most of the other items available. I took off my clothes and donned them. Then I stretched out on the bed and tried to follow Von Koerner's advice and relax.

A few moments later a girl entered. I recognized her immediately. It was five years since I'd last seen her, but Carrie Cromwell wasn't the kind of female I'd forget.

She was wearing a starched white blouse and a demure black skirt which was very full and not at all tight. Her brown hair was still in bangs and tied at the back in the manner of an old-fashioned schoolgirl. A touch of subdued lipstick was the only makeup she wore. Also, she still had that air of untouchable virtue about her—an air made paradoxical by a figure which wouldn't have been out of place coming down the runway at Minsky's.

"Hello, Mr. Victor." She greeted me calmly. "How nice to see you again."

"How nice that you remember me," I replied.

"And you me," she ping-ponged back.

"You're much more memorable than I am." I cleared

142

the net. "But perhaps this isn't the time and place to talk over old times. We have more immediate matters to discuss."

"Yes. But first I have to prepare myself for the experiment. You're ahead of me." Her lips curved in appreciation of the pajamas I'd selected. "Won't you help me decide?" She nodded toward the wardrobe closet.

"If you like."

"This one?" She took out an apricot-colored nightgown of rippling silk and held it up in front of her. "Or perhaps this?" She held up some light blue Baby Dolls. "Or do you think this might be more exciting?" She showed me a sheer black organdy, low-cut and ending just above the knee.

"They all look great to me. I guess I could never pick among them," I confessed. "You'd better decide yourself."

"All right." She took out a dark green number and lay it over the back of a chair. Then she stood up very straight and stretched. Her large breasts strained against the starched white blouse and two clear outlines marked the material over their tips.

Now Carrie lowered her arms. One of her hands went to the nape of her neck and released the clasp holding her hair in place there. She tossed her head and the copper-brown curls shimmered over her shoulders and formed a cloud framing her heart-shaped face. Her deep brown eyes, serious and intent, stared at me as she started to unbutton the blouse.

When the buttons were undone, she pulled the blouse free of the skirt and let it fall to the floor. She was wearing a full white slip with no bra under it. Her large breasts rippled against the silk, the full mounds of the upper portion of her bosom revealed above the top of the slip, a dark, intriguing shadow of deep cleavage separating them, the outline of the extended nipples and the

143

deep red of their roseates just barely discernible under the white silk.

I'd been so intent on her bosom that I hadn't noticed Carrie's hand undoing the zipper at her hip. The black skirt fell away in a wide swirl and settled to the floor. Her hands slid slowly and insinuatingly down her hips, calling my attention to the rest of her body.

It deserved all the attention I gave it. There was a subdued light coming from behind her and it made the lower part of the white slip semi-transparent. I had a sort of 'now-you-see-them-now-you-don't' view of her legs, which were long and shapely and just a little fleshy at the thighs, a touch of voluptuousness which was appealing because it seemed a subtle confirmation of her desire.

The slip hung straight from her hips, so that I could make out their shape clearly. They were wide without being bony, and their flesh trembled a little under my glance. Carrie met that glance, giggled just a bit nervously, and pirouetted once. I caught a quick flash of rosiness as the light bounced off her white silk-covered *derriere*. It was high and round and plump—everything that portion of a woman ought to be.

Now Carrie was facing me again. The light from behind her revealed just the barest suggestion of the brown triangle under her flat belly. I sensed more than saw the prickling of the soft down there.

Carrie picked up the green nightie and held it in front of her as a sort of teasing shield. She pulled it over her head and held it at her shoulders without letting it fall. She moved one of her shoulders in a voluptuous gesture and the slip strap fell away from it. She repeated the movement and the second strap was released. I caught a quick glimpse of quivering maroon nipples as the green garment replaced the white slip falling to her waist. I also caught the merest blink of that pulsating triangle as

144

the slip fell to the floor and the green nightie descended to just above Carrie's knees.

She stood before me in the nightgown now. It was quite a garment that she had selected. Made of nylon, it had wide straps which reached from her shoulders to her waist. The straps slanted inward and almost met where they ended. They had been cut away at the sides so that all but the tips of her breasts could be clearly seen. Below the waist, the center part had been cut away on either side so that the skirt was a sort of narrow triangle of cloth which revealed most of her belly—although not the navel—and left her thighs naked. In the back the straps descended even farther, to a midway point on her buttocks, so that their plumpness shimmered above the green material. Then the straps also merged to form a single triangular piece of material dangling enticingly between the backs of her thighs.

She undulated over to the bed and I grabbed for her. Hell, I'm human! But Carrie quickly danced out of reach with a little laugh. "We have to wait," she informed me.

"Wait? What for?"

"You'll see."

So I waited. It was only a few moments, but I took advantage of them to ask Carrie a few questions. My first question wasn't exactly original.

"What's a nice girl like you doing in a place like this?" I asked.

"That's too long a story to go into now," she replied. "Let's just say I'm here in the interests of science—and of keeping my husband alive."

"Then Von Koerner does have your husband?"

"Yes. He said it was all right for me to speak frankly with you. He is holding Anthony prisoner."

"Where? Here?"

"I don't know that. I doubt if he's here. That would be too risky for Von Koerner."

"Look, Carrie, I want to help you. Anthony, too. Do you believe that?"

"Yes."

"Good. Then tell me everything that happened. From the beginning. Go as far as you can before they interrupt us."

"All right. Anthony invented a mousetrap. We came to Washington so that he could patent it."

"I know about the mousetrap. The question is, how did Von Koerner find out about it?"

"I don't know that."

"All right. Go on. How did you get involved with Von Koerner?"

"That was really Anthony's doing. You know he's always been on a sort of personal crusade of his own against vice."

"I remember."

"Yes. Well, he happened to pick up this fantastic little newspaper off a newsstand. It made him see red. The whole thing was devoted to sex. Anyway, the thing that got him more than anything was the personal ads in the paper. The way he saw it, they provided a sort of carte blanche communication system for members of the sex underground. He thought there might be a chance of cracking down on them because they were using the U. S. mails. But he needed proof of their activities. That's where I came in."

"Why didn't he go after it himself?"

"He was too busy chasing around with that invention of his. Besides, he had no idea of what I was going to do. I didn't tell him. I just acted on my own. All I intended to do was a little snooping so I could give him the proof he wanted. It would have made him so happy. It's hard to explain, but Anthony's sort of a dedicated individual. He's never so happy as when he can combat the evil inside people."

"Well, that's one way to get your kicks," I observed. "But go on," I said hastily, noticing that my remark had made Carrie angry. "What exactly did you do?"

"I answered one of the ads in the paper without telling Anthony. The next thing I knew, a few days later, I got a phone call from Velvet, the bookstore proprietor. He made the arrangements for me to meet this man Barry. This Barry was—"

"I know him. Never mind that. Where did Barry take you?"

"To a party at the home of some people named George and Helen. I thought they might mind because they knew his wife and she was away. Boy, was I ever wrong! It wasn't that kind of party. Now, I'd only intended to get some evidence for Anthony. I never meant to really do anything. Honestly, up until that night, I'd never been unfaithful to Anthony." She hung her head.

"But you got carried away." I helped her out.

"Yes. But also I learned that there was much more to this sex underground than even Anthony suspected. You have to try to understand this. I felt so guilty over having been disloyal to Anthony that when Barry asked me to another sort of sex party I accepted because I really wanted to give Anthony some worthwhile evidence to sort of make it up to him. I mean, even if he didn't know—"

"It's okay. I understand. You don't have to give me any explanations." Hell, if she'd managed to rationalize it all to herself, who was I to pull the rug from under her?

"So I went with him to this spank-party, and that's where I met Von Koerner. At first he didn't seem to show any unusual interest in me, but then something must have happened. Somehow, he must have gotten wind of Anthony's invention. Anyway, he called me up at my hotel —he must have gotten the number from Velvet—and insisted I come to another party and that this time I bring my husband. I told him that was impossible and hung up. About a half-hour after that, Anthony came in. He was very upset because he'd thrown his mousetrap in the lake. Just after he came in, there was a knock at the door. It was a messenger with a package for him. As soon as I opened it, I knew it was from Von Koerner. There was a pair of leather panties in it, the same pair I'd worn at the spank-party Barry took me to. The note with them said Anthony should ask his wife their significance. Well, he did. So I told him what I'd been up to, only I lied about participating. I showed him the ad I answered and told him how Von Koerner wanted us to come to another party that evening. He wanted to go. To tell the truth, I guess I wanted him to go, too. I love Anthony, but he's so bottled up inside himself. I guess I had some sort of crazy idea that this might help him get rid of some of his repressions."

"And that's where Von Koerner grabbed him?" I speeded her along because there were people entering the chamber in which we were talking.

"Yes. He kidnapped him. And ever since he's been blackmailing me into doing whatever he wants by threatening to kill Anthony if I don't. He's had me participating here with a couple of other men who were interested in Anthony. A Chinese and—"

"What other men? Tell me—" It was too late. The four white-coated attendants, two men and two women, were upon us.

The two men took charge of me. They were most efficient. The spread was whisked off the bed and I was stretched out. Moistened rubber electrodes were attached to the soles of my feet. Another set was connected to my temples. A third was slipped inside my pajama pants and fastened to the area of my groin. Then I was neatly flipped over on my stomach. I hadn't been aware of it, but there was a small hole in the seat of my pajamas. A thermometer was neatly inserted via the aperture. There was a wire leading from it, as there was from each of the electrodes.

The pair of female attendants had wired Carrie in similar fashion. Now the four of them turned to the instrument panels lining the walls and made a series of adjustments. As they marched out the lights dimmed in the "bedroom" and starlight and moonlight trickled through the "window." Somewhere a stereo softly played the love music form *Tristan and Isolde*. A gentle but aphrodisiac perfume wafted past my nostrils.

"They don't miss a trick, do they?" I remarked.

"Everything has been prepared scientifically to provide the utmost stimulation," Carrie murmured.

"Well, you don't have to go through with this," I assured her. "There's no reason—"

"Oh, but I must! I owe it to Anthony!"

"I'm sure Von Koerner won't harm Anthony if you don't. He doesn't care if—"

"I know my duty," Carrie said fervently. "I'm here to be violated, and that's that. And you're supposed to violate me."

"Yeah, but—"

"Am I that unappealing?"

"No, but—"

"Then don't say another word." She sealed my lips with a kiss. It was quite a kiss. It left no doubt about the volcano of desire seething inside her.

Like I said before, I'm human. With her body hot and quivering against mine, who was I to re-write the script? To tell the truth, it never entered my mind. I reacted purely by instinct. I reached into the convenient slit of the nightie and caressed her bare breast.

Carrie's skin was warm, and velvet to the touch. My fingers sought out the sensitive area of her breast. I traced my finger over it and squeezed gently. It was as

149

resilient as foam rubber with a hard center of passion. "How beautiful," I murmured.

"That," Carrie informed me, "is the electrode. It's made of rubber with a metal center."

Well, I wasn't the first man to get my sex stimuli confused. Such is the age in which we live. Many a foam rubber bra has fooled a man to the point of arousal. I moved my hand, and encountered something that felt like the real thing. Still, I wasn't taking any chances. "Is that it?" I asked Carrie.

"That," she sighed, "is most definitely it!"

It swelled between my fingers as if to confirm what she said. Her hips moved in response to the touch. Her hand slid up my inner thigh, the fingers trailing excitingly up the back of my leg to my haunches. She squeezed them gently.

"Ouch!" I jumped.

"What's the matter?"

"That damn thermometer."

"Oh. Sorry." Carrie's hand relaxed its pressure.

We kissed again. The tip of her breasts was burning between my fingers now. Her hand, caressing my thighs intimately, was also hot and a trifle moist.

"What do we need these clothes for?" Her voice was husky, her lips tingling at my ear.

We took them off carefully—very carefully! It was a project, doing it so as to avoid snarling the wires. Finally we were naked, and I took Carrie in my arms again. Our lips met. Her hands turned into a fist and grasped my manhood. There was the sudden jarring note of a bell ringing.

"What was that?" My head shot up from the pillow. "What?"

"That bell. Didn't you hear it?"

"Oh, that." Carrie shrugged and pulled me to her once

150

again. "That always happens. Don't let it bother you. You'll get used to it."

"That I doubt." I slid my hand down her belly. It was soft and warm and then, as my fingers slid lower, it was furry. They slid still lower and a bright amber light blinked from one of the machines and momentarily blinded me. "I suppose that always happens, too," I commented.

"Yes. Forget about it. You're too tense. Concentrate on me, on what you're doing."

"It's like making love in the Gilbert Hall of Science."

Carrie giggled. "Or in Frankenstein's laboratory. But forget it. Just make your mind a blank and let yourself go."

It was good advice, and I took it. I gave myself up completely to sensation. I felt her quivering response as I located the fulcrum of her womanhood, and I responded back. Both her fists circled me now, and she was moaning low in her throat. Her body began to thrash about with desire, and I found myself moving with an ageless rhythm as my own passion mounted to match hers.

Her nails raked my back, urging me over her. I raised myself up and then plunged down hard. She rose up to meet my thrust.

"Ahh!" Carrie held me prisoner for a moment. Then, slowly, she began to move—little circular movements, not wild, but intense and controlled.

I followed her motions, moving slowly, horizontally, holding myself back to enjoy the exquisite tactile sensation as she both rotated and squeezed at the same time. Shudders began to sweep over her body. I leaned forward, increasing the inner pressure. That did it. She gave a little cry, and then she was heaving and bouncing beneath me like a maddened volcano about to erupt.

It was a struggle now, a wild, angry struggle. Our bodies hammered at one another like frenzied animals in a battle to the death. She screamed, and I cursed.

"Now!" Carrie screamed again. "Now! Now! Now! Rape me, you lover! Now! Rape me! Now! Give it to me now! Now! Now! Now!" Her teeth tore at my shoulder.

I grabbed her by the ears and slammed home in one final surge of berserk passion. She rose to meet it. Together we crashed through the void and split the universe apart!

A sudden sharp crackling of electricity brought us down out of that void. We'd gotten our wires crossed— literally. In our frenzied passion, we'd broken connections and tangled them. And now there were sparks shooting from our groins and the sputtering of live wires around our pubic hair.

"Don't move!" The voice boomed out from a loudspeaker somewhere in the room. "If you do, you may electrocute yourselves! Don't move! The slightest shift of position could mean the end of your lives!"

Yeah! But what a way to go!

chapter
TEN

"Wow!" Carrie hadn't quite come down out of the clouds yet. "That was the—" She caught up with our electrifying predicament. "Eek!"

"Don't move!" I cautioned her, echoing the loud-speaker, which she obviously hadn't heard.

She didn't move. Neither did I. We waited. It seemed like an eternity, but in reality, I suppose it was only a couple of minutes. Then Von Koerner appeared at the head of a phalanx of white-coated technicians. They began yanking levers and pulling wires, and finally the electrical crackling at the juncture of our bodies subsided. Gingerly, Carrie and I pulled away from each other.

Von Koerner was all apologies. I could believe his sincerity. I was the goose on the verge of laying one hundred thousand golden eggs for him and it didn't figure that he was trying to kill me. When he got through begging my pardon, he delicately broached the subject.

"Do you believe now that I have the item you wish to purchase?" Von Koerner asked.

"It seems reasonable to assume that you do."

"And you will have the money agreed upon for me tonight?"

"Yes. Providing you can assure delivery."

"I can."

I pulled on the last of my clothes. "Say, Von Koerner, will you tell me one thing?" I asked curiously.

"Perhaps. What is it you wish to know?"

"Why this whole elaborate sex bit with Mrs. Cromwell? Surely you could have just produced her, had her tell me you had her husband, and let it go at that."

"Two reasons." Von Koerner looked positively coy. "First of all, since you are the man from O. R. G. Y., I could not resist showing off our operation to you. Secondly, the lady demanded it. She remembers you from some past meeting, it seems. She positively refused to cooperate under any other circumstances. As a matter of fact, she was positively callous about her husband's fate."

"Well, I'll be damned!" I stared at Carrie Cromwell. She blushed. "I just had to—just once."

"No apologies necessary," I assured her.

I gave her a quick kiss, and we parted. Von Koerner had me escorted out of the Institute. Still vibrating a bit from the high-voltage scare I'd had, I hopped along back to my hotel.

There were the usual messages from Hortense. I was just flushing them down the toilet when the phone rang. I picked it up and said "Hello, Hortense" into the mouthpiece.

"How did you know it was me?"

"Elementary. You haven't had time to go through today's roll of dimes yet."

"What? Oh, never mind. What I called you about, Steve, was the—"

"Wedding." I finished the sentence for her.

"Oh, then it's been on your mind, too."

154

"Constantly."

"I'm so glad." Hortense missed my sarcasm. "Because we have this problem. I've inquired all over Washington, and I haven't been able to find a Zoroastran minister anywhere. How do you think your mother would feel about a Zen Buddhist?"

"Perplexed."

"Umm. I was afraid of that. I met this Zen disciple and he tried to convince me there was a similarity, but I had my doubts. You see, he was a lay person."

"Is that how you met him?"

"What?"

"Never mind."

"All right. Anyway, Steve, I'm at my wits' end. Do you think maybe your Mom might consider a Yoga?"

"I don't think so. Generally speaking, she's prejudiced against anything chiropractic."

"Well then, what are we going to do about her?"

"Let's not ask her."

"Not ask her?" Hortense was shocked. "To her own son's wedding?"

"She never liked me much, anyway."

"Really? You never told me you had Oedipal difficulties."

"I don't like to talk about it. It makes me feel guilty."

"You mean you—!" Now Hortense was really shocked.

"Constantly."

"With your own mother!"

"We were very close."

"I can imagine! But—"

"No buts. It was over a long time ago. I never think of it any more—except maybe on Mother's Day."

"What about Father's Day?"

"I spend that in a Zoroastran temple—repenting."

"Well, it's your family," Hortense said philosophically.

155

"If you don't want your own mother at the wedding—"

"I don't even want her along on the honeymoon," I assured her.

"Okay. But there's something else, Steve. The business of the maid of honor. I thought of asking Trixie."

"Who's Trixie?"

"One of the girls I used to work with. But if you have any objections—"

"None at all. Ask Trixie. As a matter of fact, why not ask the whole gang to be bridesmaids?"

"Gee, they'd love that. If you really wouldn't mind—"

"Not in the least."

"Thanks, Steve. Gosh, there are a lot of other things I have to discuss with you about the wedding."

"Why not let it go until tonight? We can talk about them then."

"How can we? We'll be with Barry and Elsa. And they already think we're married. Remember?"

"That's right. Well then, after we split from Barry and Elsa."

"We'll be at that spank-party then."

"After the party. I really don't have time now to—"

"All right. I guess it can wait if you're busy." Hortense sounded only a little bit miffed. "But I did want to ask you about the party. Do I have to go to it?"

"Sure. Don't you want to?"

"Not really. I mean, that sort of thing, now that I'm almost a married lady—it doesn't seem right."

"Well, this'll probably be the last time," I consoled her.

"Even so, it makes me feel so unfaithful—to you."

"I'm not the jealous type. Anyway, you're doing it for me."

"All right, then. I'll see you later."

"See you later." I hung up.

I just had time to shower and get dressed before the

messenger from Putnam arrived. He brought the money at seven o'clock, right on schedule. It was all in small bills, as Von Koerner had requested. I opened the package and riffled the banknotes. Money has a soothing effect on me, and this was more money than I'd ever had in my hands in my life. I sighed, re-tied the package, took it down to the lobby, put it in the hotel safe, and went out to dinner.

It was about eight-thirty when I picked it up again and left the hotel for the evening. An hour later I was on my way to Von Koerner's spank-party with Hortense, Barry and Elsa. We were in Barry's car.

"Only a few more days," Hortense whispered in my ear, squeezing my hand intimately.

Elsa saved me from having to whisper an answer. "What have you got in that package, Steve?" she asked. Her voice was pleasant, polite, friendly; it was as if she'd never come to my hotel room the night before.

"A little present for our host," I told her.

"Really? I hope it's something utilitarian. Like a new cat o' nine tails, or some pincers suitable for red-hotting."

"Oh, it's utilitarian all right," I assured her. "It's about the most utilitarian thing there is."

"Well, here we are," Barry interrupted, pulling the car up beside a veranda running alongside a large parking lot.

We got out, and an attendant took the car. A second attendant ushered us from the veranda to the entrance of the large mansion from which it extended. Here a third attendant took over and led us inside.

This third one was something to behold. He was dressed in purple livery and wore a powdered wig. Still, I guess he fit right in with the decor of the place.

It was massive. Oiled walnut and elaborate—if somewhat murky—tapestries predominated. I took a closer look at one of the tapestries. The scene woven into it harked back to the Spanish Inquisition and showed a man being drawn and quartered in detail.

We passed a huge circular staircase leading to the upper portion of the mansion, and then the footman—if that's what he was—held aside a curtain so that we might enter the main room. Big? You could have lost the Ringling Bros. circus there and still had enough space left over for the Mets to play the Dodgers. Von Koerner spotted us, detached himself from a small group of people, and came downfield to greet us. We shook hands at about second base.

"I am so glad that you could come." He included all four of us in his greeting. "Have you brought me a gift, Mr. Victor?" He eyed the package tucked securely under my arm. "How nice." He held out his hand.

"Later." I smiled at him. "I want you to have it at just the right moment. I wouldn't want to spoil things by being premature."

"And when will the right moment be?"

"When all the special guests I'm sure you've asked are present," I told him.

"What the devil are you two talking about?" Barry asked.

"Just a little secret between Mr. Victor and myself," Von Koerner told him smoothly. "Don't trouble yourself about it. Why don't you all make yourselves comfortable on this divan here? The entertainment will begin in a moment or two. When it's over," he added pointedly, speaking directly to me, "we can have a chat about just the proper circumstances for opening my gift."

Von Koerner moved off, and the four of us sat down as Von Koerner had suggested. A minute later the lights went out, and a spotlight sprang up from the ceiling to illuminate an area like a center arena. A loud scream focussed our attention on the center of the area.

Gretchen was lying there on her back, wearing a simple black wool dress with buttons down the front. Large as she was, she looked even larger stretched out that way. Under the black wool, her breasts reached for the ceiling like twin outsize missiles ready to be launched. It took a moment before I appreciated the cause of her scream.

Then I saw it. One of her bare feet was locked in a metal "boot," one of the oldest of torture weapons. The screw of the boot had just been tightened by a shapely brunette wearing a skimpy bikini made of leather and a domino mask.

There were three other brunettes, similarly attired, spaced farther away from Gretchen, as if to mark three of the four corners of a square. Now the brunette dropped the "boot" and fell back to the fourth corner. Gretchen continued to moan.

There were various paraphernalia at each of the corners, beside each of the brunettes. Now, in ritual fashion, each of them picked up a small metal bucket in one hand and a scoop in the other. With perfect timing, they simultaneously scooped burning coals from the bucket and tossed them at Gretchen. The shower of sizzling yellow-red nuggets with their black centers resulted in four geometrically perfect arcs. Gretchen screamed again, then writhed frantically to brush them off herself.

I was beginning to appreciate that Von Koerner was getting his revenge for Gretchen's attempt to double cross him with me. I also suspected that there was a reason for having me witness her punishment. It was Von Koerner's none-too-subtle way of telling me I'd better not cross him.

Of course, I had to keep in mind that he really enjoyed this sort of thing. I doubted that Gretchen did. She might

159

have dug a little mild sadism, but I judged that her pain was too intense to leave room for any erotic appreciation of it.

The four brunettes had each struck a large kitchen match now. They advanced on her in the same routinized way, half-covered buttocks bouncing in cadence, breasts swaying to some unheard rhythm. Gretchen's eyes were very wide as she watched them coming.

The first bent over and unbuttoned one button at the center of Gretchen's dress, pulling back the material to bare the navel. Then she took the flaming match and stubbed it out there. The other three followed suit. Then all four wheeled and returned to their respective corners, their tongues licking their lips in unison.

Beside me a hand squeezed my thigh. I glanced to the side and saw Elsa's eyes glittering as she stared at Gretchen. "Isn't it exciting?" she chirped. "Ooh! I can just imagine how she feels!"

"A little like a shish-ka-bob," I muttered.

"What?" Elsa's hand moved higher up my thigh.

"Skip it." I turned my attention back to the show, and so did she.

The first brunette had advanced from her corner and was removing the "boot" from Gretchen's foot now. As she returned, the Amazonian blonde sat up and massaged the red and swollen member. But her respite was brief.

All four of the masked torturers advanced on her again. Each of them had a sort of metal reel with a wire loop extending from each one. The loops were placed around Gretchen's wrists and ankles. They were drawn tight. The two tethering her wrists snagged the material of her dress. All four girls returned to their corners with the reels, letting out the metal wire as they went.

The reels were set down on the tile floor. In each corner, the tile had been removed so that the reels were embedded firmly. In concert, the brunettes began drawing the wires tighter. They stopped for just a moment when Gretchen was completely spread-eagled.

I realized I was watching a modern version of the ancient torture of drawing and quartering. Gretchen tossed her long blonde curls wildly as each of her tormentors tautened the wires another notch. Then another . . . And another . . .

She seemed beyond screaming. Her eyes bulged, her mouth strained, but no sound came out. Another notch, and the sleeves of her dress stretched so that the buttons down the front of it popped. Her breasts sprang free, the rigid nipples seeming but an additional proof of the tension pulling at her limbs. They were mammoth and trembling, like outsize balloons wafted by a gentle breeze.

Another half-notch, and now her legs seemed almost at right angles to her body. The skirt of the dress was up over her thighs. Her thigh muscles bulged as if they were at the snapping point. She wasn't wearing anything under the dress. That was obvious now. Another notch, and there was the evidence that she was a natural blonde. Parting this evidence was the flesh of her womanhood drawn so tightly back that the treasure-cave it flanked was almost completely revealed.

One more tightening of the reels. The material of the dress tore away from her body. She was naked now. A rivulet of perspiration ran down the deep cleft between her breasts, collected in her blistered navel, then overflowed to moisten the blonde triangle. Another notch, and that did it. Gretchen fainted.

Von Koerner strode to the center of the arena. He held an ice bucket in his hands. He poised directly over her and overturned the bucket. Shaved ice cascaded onto her face.

It did the trick. She whimpered and opened her eyes. She was conscious again.

Von Koerner held up a hand to signal the four brunettes not to carry the torture any further. "Gentlemen," he announced, "the time has come to take your pleasure. One at a time, if you please."

A short, fat man in a tuxedo came forward. He removed his pants and shorts. He fell on Gretchen, wheezing and grunting his lust.

Immediately the four masked girls went into ritualized action. Whips in their hands, they advanced on the pair and lashed out in cadence. Two of them drew blood from the fat posterior of the eager man. The other two concentrated on Gretchen's breasts.

Finally the fat man was finished. He scampered off, and the four furies stood back. A younger man, a Charles Atlas type, advanced. His naked legs and haunches bulged with muscles. He went at Gretchen brutally. Once again the four whips cracked out.

Another man, and another. Each time the same ritualized beating repeated. By the time Barry advanced to take his turn, Gretchen's breasts were bleeding.

"Ooh! Isn't Barry wonderful?" Elsa's nails dug into my crotch.

I was too disgusted to answer. I pulled away and watched silently. Beside me Hortense was covering her eyes.

"Aren't you going to take a turn, Steve?" Barry asked when he returned.

"No," I told him shortly.

He looked at me curiously and shrugged. I realized that for a supposed discipline advocate I must seem to him to be lacking in enthusiasm. The hell with it! Let him think whatever he wanted to think.

Finally it was over. Gretchen, only half-conscious, was carried out by her four tormentors. The spotlight went out, and the room lights went back on. Von Koerner came straight to me and guided me toward an alcove where we could talk privately.

"Did you enjoy the exhibition, Mr. Victor?" he asked as we crossed the room.

"No!" I told him shortly.

"I'm so sorry. And I planned it so carefully. I wanted something extra-special because this is, after all, a farewell celebration. However, even if you didn't enjoy it, I'm sure the others did. And Gretchen, I would say, will not forget me after I am gone."

"I'm sure she won't." It came out a snarl. I controlled my feelings. "Let's get down to business," I told him. "Where's Cromwell?"

"The amount agreed upon is in that package?"

"Yes."

"Then give it to me and I will direct you to Cromwell."

"Nothing doing. You don't get your hands on this money until I have Cromwell in person."

"I was afraid you would take that attitude. Very well, then. Much as your distrust pains me, we'll do it your way. I will take you to Cromwell."

Von Koerner started to lead me from the room. Just as we reached the door, Hortense intercepted us. "Where are you going?" she wanted to know.

"Your husband and I are merely stepping out for a little while," Von Koerner told her.

"Can't I come?"

"No." I didn't know what I might be getting into. I didn't want to have to worry about Hortense as well as Cromwell and myself.

"I don't want to stay here alone," she pouted. "I told you how I felt."

I looked at Von Koerner questioningly.

"Let her come," he said. "It makes no difference."

We went out the front way. Von Kerner had a servant bring his car around. It was quite a car—a new Dodge Charger, black, and equipped to the teeth. With Von

Koerner at the wheel, it purred off like a pussycat. I sat in front with him, floating in the bucket seat. Hortense sat in back.

Von Koerner guided the car back along the route we'd taken with Barry before. He threw the stick shift into overdrive and we hummed along at sixty. It was a soft ride despite the sure road feel of the car under me.

We slowed down as we passed through the center of Washington. The Lincoln Memorial, the White House, the Washington Monument—we glided past them all. Then we were approaching rock Creek Park. For a crazy minute it occurred to me that Von Koerner might have Cromwell stashed away at the very hotel from which he'd vanished—my hotel.

But we passed it, and soon we were out on the open road again. We veered northwest and crossed over into Maryland, somewhere between Silver Spring and Chevy Chase. The landscape was sprinkled with upper-class houses on both sides of us, but the particular road Von Koerner was wheeling the Charger down was fairly deserted. He pulled off it onto a dirt road, rounded a grove of trees, and touched the control of the four-wheel disc brakes so that the Charger slid to a smooth stop beside a deserted looking shack.

We got out. "He's in there," Von Koerner told me. He held out his hand for the package with the money in it.

"Let's see him." I kept a firm grip on the package.

"You are too suspicious, Mr. Victor. I assure you that I am acting in good faith." He reached in his pocket, took out a gun, pointed it at me, and smiled. "I could shoot you right now and take the money," he pointed out.

"You wouldn't get very far," I assured him. "You'd bring the whole U. S. government down on you."

"Exactly. I don't want that. I am prepared to go through with the transaction exactly as planned. To prove it, I will leave my weapon out here—providing that you do the same."

"All right." I took my gun from my shoulder holster and handed it to Hortense. "Take this and wait in the car," I told her. "If our friend here is trying to pull a fast one and comes out without me, shoot to kill. And don't miss."

"Steve, I don't know what this is all about, but—"

"There's no time to explain now. Just do as I say."

"All right." Hortense got into the car.

I followed Von Koerner to the shack, still holding onto the money. He produced a key, opened a large padlock, and removed the chain which had ringed the door. He also had to remove an iron bar before the door could swing open.

It was pitch black inside. I motioned to Von Koerner to go first. He reached inside the door and groped. I guessed there must have been some sort of shelf there. Finally he came up with a flashlight. He turned it on and aimed the beam low at the far side of the shack.

Standing at his elbow, I made out a cot there. There was a figure lying on it. As I followed Von Koerner inside the shack, I saw that the figure was tied to the cot. My eyes traveled upward to the face. There was adhesive tape over the mouth. Even so, and despite the years since I'd last seen him, I had no difficulty recognizing Anthony Bowdler Cromwell.

"The money, please," Von Koerner said.

It occurred to me that there wasn't one damn reason why I should give it to him at this point. The flashlight beam flicked to my face, and he must have read what I was thinking there. He took a step away from me and aimed the beam at Cromwell again. His other hand hovered over Cromwell's throat. There was an ice-pick in it. The flashlight wasn't the only thing Von Koerner had taken from the shelf.

So now I had the reason to pay him. I handed him the money. Still holding the icepick, he moved to the door. "You can untie him now." Von Koerner motioned towards Cromwell. "I'll wait here and you can go out first. I wouldn't want the young lady to leap to any wrong conclusions and get trigger-happy. Then you can take my car. I've made other arrangements."

The adhesive tape over Cromwell's mouth was virtually embedded in his flesh. I had to pick at it a little at a time to get it off. His eyes told me the process was painful. Also, the knots of the ropes binding him had been soaked in water and it was going to be a painstaking business working them loose. That icepick Von Koerner would have come in handy, but I knew he wouldn't give it to me.

As I worked over Cromwell, I tossed a few questions at Von Koerner. He wasn't at all reticent about answering them. I guess he figured he had nothing to lose. He'd gotten what he wanted and was all set to remove himself from the action. It didn't matter what he told me now. Also, Von Koerner was naturally a braggart. He enjoyed crowing about his scheme and how well he'd executed it.

As he talked, while I worked over Cromwell, the pieces of the puzzle, the missing pieces Von Koerner now provided, fell neatly into place. One piece of luck, a coincidence, had placed von Koerner in the position he was now so thoroughly enjoying, the position which had netted him the hundred grand he now clutched in his hot little hand. This coincidence was personified by Carrie Cromwell.

But the scheme itself had begun not with her, but with Knute Hajstrom. Von Koerner had known Hajstrom many years ago in Europe. After the war, Von Koerner had "found it necessary" to "emigrate" to Stockholm from his native Germany. By this I guessed that he had probably been on some list of wanted Nazi scientists and had managed to get out one jump ahead of the War Crimes Commission. In any case, since he had no license to practice medicine in Sweden, he had been forced to do so illicitly. He practised a peculiar form of gynecology in Stockholm's nether world of sex. The Swedes have a very permissive attitude toward sex. Abortion, for instance, is legal. But they do draw the line at groups which go in for certain specialized perversions. It was to these groups that Von Koerner catered. He performed operations to sensitize the sex organs, operations which left the patient in the perpetual state of one who takes aphrodisiacs regularly. He also devised and sold various gadgets to heighten the sex experience. And he patched up occasional victims of discipline club parties which had gotten out of hand.

That's where Hajstrom came into the picture. He was an ardent follower of the De Sade theory of combining sex with pain. He brought a very young girl to Von Koerner one night. The girl had been brutally beaten by him. She was unconscious and bleeding internally. Despite Von Koerner's ministrations, she died. Von Koerner disposed of the body for Hajstrom.

Even in those days Hajstrom was a prominent engineer. Learning this, Von Koerner started blackmailing him. Hajstrom came from a very wealthy family. Shortly after the incident with the girl, his father died and he came into a great deal of money. Von Koerner relieved him of a substantial portion of it and came to the United States.

Here Von Koerner played it straight for a short while. He served his internship, took his medical boards, and was licensed to practice as a gynecologist. Then, using what was left of the money he had extorted from Hajstrom, he had founded the Research Institute of Advanced Gynecology. Once it was established, he had found it easy to get wealthy individuals and foundations to invest in it. Recently he had pulled out his original investment, sold his interest at a profit, and made arrangements to disassociate himself from the Institute and its research program.

He had begun to make these arrangements when he learned that Hajstrom was in Washington, on loan from the University of Stockholm to the U. S. government as an expert in alloys with much valuable knowledge pertaining to our outer space program. He had started blackmailing Hajstrom again. But the well had almost run dry, and he recognized that he could only get so much before he drove the Swede to suicide. This was how things stood when Cromwell came into the picture.

One look at Cromwell's mousetrap and Hajstrom had recognized the value of the alloy used in its creation immediately. He must have thought he saw the glimmering of a way to get Von Koerner off his back. In any case, he called Von Koerner before he went to the Pentagon and told them of Cromwell's discovery.

"It was I who decided he should alert the Pentagon," Von Koerner told me smugly.

"Why did you do that?" I asked.

"Because I knew I would have Cromwell in my possession before they could get to him. And I thought they would pay handsomely to get him back. As it turns out, they have. But if they hadn't, there were other governments who were interested."

The reason Von Koerner had been so sure of himself was Carrie Cromwell. Originally she'd been brought to one of his spank-parties by Barry. But she'd gotten to Barry through Velvet, and Von Koerner was the power behind Velvet. The bookseller was a front, as was the bookshop, for another of Von Koerner's schemes. He had compiled information about all the people who had dealt with Velvet and been steered into underground sex activities. His purpose was blackmail.

Thus Von Koerner had made it his business to know all about Carrie Cromwell and her husband. With Anthony Bowdler Cromwell such a bluenose, he had thought he might eventually blackmail Carrie, or perhaps even Cromwell himself. Then had come the call from Hajstrom about Cromwell's discovery, and Von Koerner had seen the opportunity for some really big money.

He had called Carrie and insisted she bring her husband to the spank-party that evening. When she balked, he sent the note with the leather panties to Cromwell. That did it. Cromwell fell into his hands like a ripe plum.

After that he had put out feelers to the various governments, letting Hajstrom's contact with the Pentagon serve as the contact for the U. S. government. Then he had played a waiting game, figuring that would push the price up. But when Hajstrom had been killed, he'd decided to wait no longer.

"Your killing Hajstrom made me nervous," he admitted. "Was that your purpose?"

I didn't answer him. I guessed that my Russian double had killed Hajstrom because Hajstrom was the competition. Also he must have known I'd be blamed for it, and that would not only make trouble for me with the police, but would also make Von Koerner suspicious, which it had. But his greed was greater than his suspicion, and so here we were.

I had Cromwell untied now. He got to his feet. He was pretty wobbly. I gave him a minute to get hold of himself. That minute proved costly.

Von Koerner was standing to one side of the door, his

back to it. The beam from his flashlight was in my eyes. He had the packet of money under his arm, the icepick still in his hand.

Then, suddenly, he stiffened, his face crumpled with agony, and he pitched forward to the floor. The flashlight went spinning crazily out of his grasp. Something hard hit me on the side of the head. It didn't knock me unconscious, but it dazed me for a moment. I was still dazed as I stumbled to the door and tripped over Von Koerner's body.

As if through a fog, I saw Cromwell shoved into the rear seat of the Charger. The door was slammed behind him, and I saw the face of the man who'd been shoving him. My mind struggled with the perception that it was Stevkovsky, my double.

"Von Koerner tried to pull a fast one," I heard him say to Hortense as he ran around to the driver's side of the car. "He'll be after us, so let's go. I'll drive."

"Hey, wait a—" I tried to shout as the car pulled away. It came out a weak whisper.

I got up and saw the knife sticking out of Von Koerner's back. It shocked me back into awareness. My mind raced with the import of what had happened. Stevkovsky must have been tailing us. He'd probably parked his car down the dirt road and sneaked up to the cabin on foot. It was dark out, and he'd probably moved fast, so Hortense hadn't seen him. Now she thought that he was me again. I couldn't guess what Cromwell might be thinking. He'd been pretty dazed himself. Chances are that with everything happening so quickly, he probably thought Stevkovsky was me, too.

I relieved the corpse of the packet of money. I was recovered now and I started moving fast. I'd probably waited too long, but still I had to try to catch the Charger. I darted down the dirt road until I spotted

170

the car Stevkovsky had left there. It was a Porsche road-ster with a convertible top. I was still holding the knife I'd taken out of Von Koerner's back. I slashed the top of the Porsche, reached inside, and opened it. It was the work of less than a minute to cross the wires under the ignition and start it up.

I bounced down the rutty dirt road with all the speed I could milk out of the Porsche. Where it met the high-way I stopped and found the tire tracks of the Charger veering left just before they vanished on the pavement. Stevkovsky was heading away from Washington.

I turned left, shifted the gears fast, went into over-drive, and did my best to push the pedal through the floorboard. Luck was with me. Five minutes later I saw lanterns marking a construction detour coming up in the distance. Just as I saw them, the Charger came around a bend heading in the opposite direction.

Stevkovsky had goofed. He didn't know the area. He'd made a wrong guess when he turned. Now he was retracing his route.

The Porsche tires skidded as I made a high-speed U turn and took off after him. He must have spotted me in the rear-view mirror. He really poured on the gas, and the Charger leaped ahead. I was pushing the Porsche as fast as it would go again, but it wasn't fast enough. It was all I could do to keep the tail-lights of the Charger in sight as it whipped around the curves.

Fortunately, the Charger ran into traffic as it pulled onto one of the main roads leading back from Maryland into Washington. It weaved in and out, sure as a moun-tain goat, but I managed to keep it in sight. Then we were out of the traffic again, heading up into the hills on the north side of Rock Creek Park.

The Charger took the hairpin turns as if it was on rails. I followed in the Porsche, my tires squealing under me, glad of its sure balance, but wishing it had a little more oomph. If we hit a straightaway, the Charger could lose me easily.

But it wasn't a straightaway that undid me. It was a sudden steep grade. A mountain—or maybe only a large hill—rising up on my right, the sharp drop of a ravine on my left, I milked the downhill stretch for all the speed I could get in an effort to close the distance with the Charger. At the bottom of the grade, it made a sharp right turn and vanished from sight.

As I hit the bottom, I too swung into a right-hand turn. Too late, I saw that the road immediately cut back left again. I oversteered. There was the sound of crunching wood as the Porsche hit the fence separating the road from the ravine head-on. The little sports car soared into the air, and then plunged downwards toward the black pit yawning below.

chapter
ELEVEN

THE PORSCHE landed on an outcropping of rocks and burst into flames. I landed on my rear end and kept going at a high speed that ripped the seat of my pants completely away. Fortunately, the car and I had parted company before either of us landed.

At the moment that the Porsche hit the railing, I had hit the door and jumped free. I was no longer in it as it soared toward the abyss. I'd slid to a halt and was grabbing to see if my rump was still there by the time the resulting fire lit up the sky. I was still gingerly trying to investigate the damage to my fundament when I spotted headlights coming back up the road from the direction in which I'd been headed. Just on a hunch, I got behind some bushes at the side of the road.

It was a good thing I did. It was the Charger, all right. I guess Stevkovsky was checking to see if he was finally rid of me. It slowed as it passed me, without completely stopping.

"He must have been killed," I heard Hortense say. "Poor Dr. Von Koerner."

"He tried to kill me," Stevkovsky reminded her, lying.

"But I guess he's dead, all right." From the smug tone of his voice, I knew that I was the one he thought had perished in the Porsche.

The Charger picked up speed and purred away. I came out from behind the bushes and started walking. There was nothing else to do.

It must have been two hours before I found my way out of the Rock Creek area. I spotted a bar on a side street and went into it to use the telephone. As I walked the length of the place to the back where the phone booths were, a drunk swiveled around on his barstool and eyed my protruding posterior.

"Jush wha' kinda joint is this?" He demanded of the bartender. "I thought ya din serve queers."

"He didn't ask to be served." The bartender shrugged it off.

"Ain't it kinna breezhy goin' aroun' like that?" the drunk called after me.

"Kiss my ass!" I told him.

"Shee!" he exclaimed to the bartender. "I gotta six sense. I alwaysh know a fairy when I see one!" He got off his stool and followed me to the back.

He reached the phone booth just as I was dialing Putnam's number. He made a "shame-shame" gesture and shook his head at me. I stuck my tongue out at him, and he turned even redder than he was.

"Hello?" Putnam answered the phone.

"Steve Victor here," I identified myself.

"Again? What do you want now? I just got off the phone with you."

"If you just got off the phone with somebody, it wasn't me."

"Didn't you just get through telling me how Von Koerner outwitted you and almost escaped with the money and with Cromwell. Didn't you just tell me how Von

174

Koerner and Cromwell and the money all went up in flames when the car they were in crashed?"

"I didn't call you," I said firmly. "That must have been Stevkovsky."

"Wait a minute! How do I know you're not Stevkovsky?"

"American original."

"Okay. Okay, Steve. Now you'd better tell me exactly what did happen."

I told him. Just as I was finishing, the drunk tapped on the glass of the phone booth. I opened the door a crack.

"Come on out and fight, ya dirty queer!" He held up a fist threateningly.

"I'm a lover, not a fighter," I informed him.

"What? What did you say?" Putnam was confused.

"Never mind. What do you suppose Stevkovsky's next move will be?"

"As I see it, he figures you're dead and intends to go on impersonating you for a while. He's staying at your room. And he's evidently planning to go ahead and marry your fiancee. He asked me not to give him any more assignments for a while so they could go on their honeymoon."

"I'll be damned! What do you suppose his angle is?"

"I just don't know," Putnam admitted.

"What about Hortense? And Cromwell? What did he do with them?"

"I don't know that, either. But I'll put some men on it. You'd better get back to me later, Steve. After I see what we can find out."

"Okay." I hung up and opened the door to the phone booth. The drunk was waiting for me.

"Come out of there and fight like a man, you pansy!" He held up both fists and weaved, snorting loudly.

"I'm not a pansy." I stayed seated in the phone booth. I was just too damn tired to fight.

"Then how come you're advertising that way with your bare rear end hanging out?"

"I'm really a vice cop," I told him in a low, conspiratorial tone. "I'm out to lure fruits so we can nail them."

"No kidding." He was impressed. "Anything I can do to help?" He stood back and all but bowed me out of the phone booth.

"No," I told him as I started back down the bar. "But thanks for the offer, anyway."

"Gee," he bounced along at my side. "You guys are terrific. You sure could have fooled me."

"It's dear of you to say so, sweetie." I patted his cheek, gave it a little pinch, and pushed through the swinging doors.

I went down the street to the first cheap hotel in sight. After I checked in, I sent the bellhop out to buy me a pair of pants. Then I filled the tub with hot water and soaked my mistreated bottom for a good hour. Finally I crawled out of the tub, patted it dry, and hit the sack. Uncomfortable as it was sleeping on my stomach, I still slept deeply.

The first thing I did after I woke the next afternoon was call Putnam. "American original." I gave him the password so he'd know I was the one-and-only, bona-fide, dyed-in-the-wool Steve Victor.

"Here's what we've managed to piece together," he told me. "After the accident, he drove Hortense back to her hotel and dropped her off. We don't know where he went after that, but wherever it was, that must be where he's hiding Cromwell. Now he's at your hotel, posing as you. We've been tapping his wire. Most of his calls are from Hortense. He's going right ahead with the wedding plans. He's even made arrangements to rent a yacht for the honeymoon."

"A yacht?"

176

"Yes. The idea is that he and Hortense are going to sail up the Potomac."

"That must be how he plans to get Cromwell out of Washington," I deduced.

"It seems likely. He's a pretty shrewd customer. Calling me last night was really a stroke of genius. It tied up all the loose ends. If he'd been right in thinking you were dead, I would have bought his story about Cromwell dying and marked the case closed. And I would have gone to the wedding none the wiser."

"You mean you've been invited to the wedding?"

"Well, why not?" Putnam sounded a little hurt that I'd even raised the question. "After all, we have been rather closely associated for quite a while. You certainly meant to ask me, I hope. I mean, I wouldn't want to take advantage of the situation. If I'm not wanted—"

"Of course I meant to ask you," I told him soothingly. "Wouldn't think of getting married without you. I'm just surprised Stevkovsky thought of it."

"Well, even the Russians aren't all bad. They have some consideration for people's feelings even if some other people don't."

"When is the wedding?" I interrupted his brooding.

"Day after tomorrow." He mentioned the hour.

"Where?"

"In the Vedic Temple. Our wire-tap picked up a lot of talk about that. It was the closest Hortense could come to Zoroaster."

The Vedic Temple! "Okay," I told Putnam. "I'll see you in church."

There was nothing else to do for the next two days except relax and wait. I caught up on my sleep, read a lot, and only left my hotel room for quickie meals. I didn't want to take even the slightest chance of Stevkovsky or one of his cohorts spotting me. My biggest asset was for him to go on thinking I was dead.

177

Finally the big day arrived. For a bridegroom, I wasn't at all nervous. But then why should I have been? I was only being married by proxy, after all.

I'd checked out the details with Putnam. It was to be a formal affair. It hadn't been hard for him to find out what Stevkovsky was wearing, down to the last detail. I duplicated it—white tie, tails, ruffled shirt—right down to the last ruffle. Then, over the outfit, I donned a long raincoat, buttoned it up to the collar, and topped it off with a slouch hat and dark glasses.

At some point after the ceremony, during the reception, Stevkovsky would have to leave Hortense's side to make arrangements to have Cromwell transferred to the yacht. When that happened, I intended to shed my outer garments, make my appearance, and temporarily replace him. I hoped to be able to grab Hortense for a little while and pump her as to their honeymoon plans. Putnam had been unable to find out where they were boarding the yacht, or what their eventual destination was to be. If I was lucky, I'd be able to get that information in time to intercept them and rescue Cromwell once again. My final preparation for that moment was to slip a midget revolver into the raincoat pocket.

Putnam provided a closed car to transport me to the Vedic Temple. The driver pulled up around the back. His instructions were to wait there with the motor running. I waited inside the car until the noises from the front entrance of the place announced that the bride had arrived. Then I took advantage of the commotion to slip in through the back entrance.

Putnam was there waiting for me. He guided me to a small side room. "You'll be safe in here," he assured me. "It's only used for storage. And you can see both the chapel and the main room where the reception is to be held from here. All you have to do is stand on this chair and look over the transom."

"Check." I mounted the chair and verified the range offered my vision.

"I'll see you later." When I'd climbed down, he moved the chair back so he could leave the room. "Oh, and congratulations," he added. "I'm sure you'll be very happy."

Sarcastic so-and-so! I replaced the chair, climbed up again and studied the crowd. Hortense certainly had a lot of important friends. I spotted half a dozen well-known congressmen, three senators, and one Supreme Court judge. The judge's smile may have been a little stiff, but he was doing his best to be courteous to a young lady with henna-dyed hair and a low-cut gown that was just a bit too revealing for the occasion. I guessed Hortense had really gone all out in exerting some gentle pressure to tone up the proceedings.

Some of the nabobs had even brought their wives. Looking at them and contrasting them with the other ladies present—friends of Hortense, probably co-workers, I guessed—I could see why some of the men must have had reason to stray into Hortense's pasture. Alas, the wives were a dowdy lot; middle-aged spread had caught up with them, and they lacked the excitement generated by the other girls. I was reminded of Perle Mesta's remark that Washington is a town populated by the most interesting, brilliant, distinguished, influential men in the world—and the women they married when they were very young!

Finally the crowd was seated in the chapel and the wedding started. Organ music sprang up, and after a moment I watched myself—anyway, that's what it felt like—marching down the aisle to a fate worse than death —which was also what it felt like. And I'll be damned if my best man wasn't Charles Putnam!

They halted before the altar. The organ switched over to *Here Comes the Bride*, and Hortense made her appearance on the arm of a United States Senator. She looked as if she'd stepped right out of a bride's book. Her gown was white satin, her veil white tulle, and she carried a large bouquet of forget-me-nots. She might have been a casual bride to half the Washington legislators once, but right now she was every inch a real, legitimate bride, and her face bore a look of exaltation that testified of her re-virginization.

The Vedic priest began the ceremony. It was long and involved incense and candles and a lot of mumbo-jumbo in a language that was strange to me. But he switched over to English for the last part. Cold fear clutched my vitals as I heard myself saying "I do" and then watched myself kissing the bride.

Back up the aisle, bride and groom arm in arm, and then the reception began. The bride took her position and the men lined up to kiss her. Some of them came back for seconds. Then the bride vanished, gone to change to traveling clothes, I guessed. The groom was still trapped in a crowd of well-wishers.

Suddenly I saw Putnam approaching my hiding place. I got the chair out of the way so he could slip inside. "He's still being cagey," he told me. "Several people have asked him where they're going on the honeymoon, but he just laughs and plays it like a groom trying to avoid honeymoon jokers. I've been staying within earshot, but I haven't been able to learn a thing."

"All we can do is stay with it," I replied.

Putnam slipped out again, and I once again climbed up to the transom. Hortense was back mingling with the guests. She had changed into a lightweight traveling suit and looked very demure. Stevkovsky was at her elbow.

An hour went by before he left her. Then he bent, whispered something in her ear, and was gone from the scene. I moved fast to replace him, knowing that he might be back at any moment.

"So fast?" Hortense raised an eyebrow when I appeared beside her.

"I couldn't bear to be away from you for a moment, my darling."

"Oh, you are so sweet. But after all, when nature calls —I mean, I'm not that possessive!"

"It can wait," I assured her. "Besides, there's something else bothering me. You're going to think I'm an awful birdbrain, sweetheart. But the truth is that with everything that's been happening, I seem to have our plans all mixed up in my head. I know it's silly, but I wonder if you'd go over them with me." I drew her to one side so we could talk confidentially.

"Well, we're due at the yacht at four," she told me, her eyes shining. "And—"

"Where is the yacht picking us up, again? I'm so confused."

She told me. "And then we're going to spend our wedding night on the Potomac. And tomorrow morning we'll be off on our honeymoon."

"Ahh yes. Where are we going again?"

"I can't help you there, my darling. That's your surprise. Remember, you wouldn't tell me because you wanted to see my eyes shine when we arrive? But don't worry about it. You're just a nervous bridegroom, poor boy. You won't be so mixed up when we get to the yacht. Everything will come back to you."

"I'm sure it will. And now I really have to go." I'd just spotted Putnam signaling frantically to me that Stevkovsky was returning.

"Don't be long, my darling."

I darted back to my hiding place. Looking through the transom again, I watched as Stevkovsky went up to Hortense. She really looked puzzled at what must have seemed to her to be such a quick reappearance.

Putnam waited a few minutes and then rejoined me. I

told him what I had learned. "Don't descend on the dock where the yacht is picking them up with a bunch of men," I warned him. "My guess is Cromwell isn't aboard yet, and if whoever's bringing him spots anything funny, he may slip through our fingers. I'm going to head out there now and try to get aboard before the wedding couple arrives. That way I'll be ready to help Cromwell."

"All right," Putnam agreed.

I slipped out the back door of the Vedic Temple by the same route I'd used in entering. My driver was waiting with the car, the motor running. I gave him our destination, and we started out.

About twenty minutes later I had him drop me off some distance from where the yacht was moored. I didn't want to be spotted boarding it. But luck was against me.

I got down on the dock easily enough. Here I stayed out of sight behind some packing cases until there was nobody on deck. Then I made a dash up the gangplank, across the deck, and down the stairway to where I presumed the cabins would be. I took a guess and opened one of the doors. I'd guessed right. Flowers, champagne, an ice bucket—these things identified it as the cabin being held in readiness for the wedding couple. But the cabin wasn't empty!

"Why, hello, sir. We hadn't expected you until later." The gold braid on the cap worn by the middle-aged man speaking identified him as the Captain. "I was just checking to see that everything was in order for your arrival."

"Yes, yes. Very good," I stammered.

"May I extend heartiest congratulations for myself and the crew, sir?"

"Of course." I shook his hand. "Thank you."

"I'd like to congratulate the bride too, sir." The Captain peered behind me. "Is she on deck?"

"No. No, she hasn't arrived yet."

"Hasn't arrived yet?" he exclaimed.

"Yes," I improvised desperately. "We came by separate cars."

"Separate cars?" The Captain was bewildered. "That's a bit unusual for a wedding couple, isn't it, sir?"

"It's because I'm a Zoroastran," I babbled. "My creed prohibits the bride and groom riding in the same vehicle."

"A Zoroastran, eh? What a coincidence," the Captain said. "My first wife was a Zoroastran."

"Was she, now?" I boomed it out heartily to cover my confusion. "That is a coincidence. There aren't too many of us Zoroastrans around."

"No, there aren't. But after our wedding, we traveled in the same car." His voice was openly skeptical.

"Did you, now? But then I'll bet you weren't married in a Vedic Temple. That makes all the difference, you know."

"As a matter of fact, we were."

"You were?"

"Yes."

"Heh-heh. Well, now, that really is a coincidence."

"And it didn't make any difference," the Captain said firmly. "About riding in the same car, I mean."

"It didn't?"

"No."

"Oh."

"It's all right, sir." The Captain's face lit up with sudden logic. He thought he'd figured it all out. "Had a little spat, didn't you? It happens. But don't worry about it. She'll be along."

"As a matter of fact, that's exactly what happened," I admitted, leaping at the welcome out he'd provided. "But you're right. She should be here soon."

"Then I'll be leaving, sir. You'll want to be alone with her." He nudged me in the ribs. "Two's company, and three's a crowd. Especially on a honeymoon, eh, sir?" He chortled.

"You're a man of the world, Captain," I assured him as I saw him to the door and closed it behind him.

As soon as he was gone, I cased the cabin for a place to hide. There were two closets, but I decided against both of them. The nuptial couple might decide to hang up their clothes, and I'd be discovered immediately. A third door led to the bathroom. I decided against that, too. The odds were that one of them might use it.

That left only one possibility. Under the bed. It was a little French bedroom farce-y, but I had no other choice. I stationed myself at the porthole, which provided a clear view of the dock, and stood poised to dart under the bed when they arrived.

It wasn't too long a wait. A limousine pulled up and Stevkovsky and Gretchen got out of it. As they stood there brushing the rice from their clothes, a small delivery truck pulled up from the other direction. With Stevkovsky overseeing their labor, two men got out of the truck and unloaded a large packing crate from the rear.

Stevkovsky guided them up the gangplank with it. Then he left Hortense on deck alone for a few moments while he showed them where to store it. He returned and they started for the stairway. I dived under the bed.

The door to the cabin opened, and they entered. Stevkovsky was carrying Hortense across the threshold. He set her down, and they kissed.

"Oh, darling, it's so wonderful to be alone at last," Hortense murmured when the kiss was over. "I'm sure everything will come back to you now."

"Huh?"

"All the details you forgot about our honeymoon. Now that the hectic part is over, I'm sure you'll remember them."

"What are you talking about?"

"Oh, my poor darling, you really are under a strain. Don't you remember how worried you were about not recalling—" Hortense was interrupted by a discreet tapping at the door. "Who can that be?"

"Probably the Captain," Stevkovsky told her.

"Oh, darn it. Look, I'll just go into the bathroom and slip into something comfortable," she whispered insinuatingly. "You get rid of him quickly, will you, darling?"

"All right." Stevkovsky waited until she was gone and then opened the door.

"Pardon, sir. I was wondering about that crate you had in the hold," the Captain said apologetically. "One of the crew said he heard some strange noises coming from it."

"Tell the crew to keep away from that crate. That's an order, Captain."

"Very well, sir. Is it all right if we lift anchor now?"

"Yes. Let's get under way."

The Captain started out, then paused in the doorway. "I saw you drive up, sir," he said in a conspiratorial whisper. "Went to fetch her yourself, did you? Well, that's the ticket. Have to cater to them at least until the honeymoon's over, eh?" He nudged Stevkovsky in the ribs and left.

As he closed the door behind him, the look of puzzlement was still on Stevkovsky's face. He stood there a moment, scratching his head. His expression seemed to say that nobody was making any sense today.

Watching him, I decided to make my move. Cromwell was undoubtedly inside that crate. It would be best to rescue him before the yacht started down the river. There was no point in adding the possibility of a swim to the other dangers involved.

Pistol first, I pulled myself out from under the bed. I got to my feet fast, while Stevkovsky was still stunned

185

by my sudden appearance. As he recognized me, he went as white as if he'd seen a ghost. From his point of view, I suppose that's what I was.

"Is the Captain gone, darling?" Hortense's voice called from the bathroom.

I shoved the gun against Stevkovsky's belly and indicated that he should remain silent. "Not yet," I called back. "Take me to Cromwell." I pushed the gun harder against his gut.

"Don't be silly. Cromwell is dead," he bluffed.

"I know better. Remember? Now take me to wherever you stored that crate."

"What about her?" He jerked his thumb towards the bathroom door.

"I have to see to some things with the Captain, darling," I called out. "I'll be back in a few minutes."

"Well, for Pete's sake, hurry!" Hortense sounded annoyed.

I nudged Stevkovsky with the gun, and he preceded me out of the cabin. We went up the stairway and across the deck without seeing anyone. Finally we were down in the hold.

Spotting a crowbar, I picked it up and handed it to Stevkovsky. "Get to work," I told him, motioning toward the packing case.

He got to work prying off the boards in which the case itself was encased. I could hear movements inside it as he worked. Taking a closer look, I saw that airholes had been drilled in it.

At last Stevkovsky was finished. He stood back and lifted the cover of the case. When I saw the way Cromwell had been crammed into it, I was really shocked and angry. "You bastard!" I cursed my double. "You could have given him more room. You didn't have to torture him." I reached out my hand and grabbed Cromwell under one arm to help him sit up.

It was a mistake. I'd taken my eyes off Stevkovsky for just a brief instant. He was still holding the crowbar. I sensed rather than saw him swing it straight for my skull!

Flinging myself sideways, I managed to catch the blow on my shoulder. The bone snapped under the impact. Luckily, it was my left shoulder. I still had the gun in my right hand. The pain was excruciating, but I aimed it by reflex and pulled the trigger.

My face—the face of my double—contorted with shock. A hole appeared in the forehead and blood spurted from it. Stevkovsky pitched to the floor. He was dead.

I helped Cromwell out of the packing case. He was so weak his knees kept buckling under him. My shoulder hurt like hell, but I supported him with my other arm and helped him up to the deck.

All I wanted to do now was get him off the boat. There was always the chance that Stevkovsky had accomplices among the crew. I was reasonably sure that the captain was clean, but as for the other crew members, there was no telling who might be a Russian agent.

We made it down the gangplank with no trouble. I got Cromwell behind some packing cases alongside the ship and we rested there a moment. From this vantage point, I had an up-from-under angle view of the deck as Hortense appeared.

She'd thrown a coat over the nightgown she'd donned. "Steve," she called.

I couldn't see the Captain, but I heard him answering. "If you're looking for your husband, I caught a glimpse of him going down to the hold with another gentleman," he told her.

"Oh. Thank you. The hold—where is that?"

"Over there." He must have pointed.

Silence as she vanished from view. Then a scream— loud, shocked, grief-stricken. Footsteps on the deck

187

above. Commotion. Then the Captain supporting Hortense as she stumbled blindly back up the deck.

"Dead," she sobbed. "I can't believe it. On our wedding day. We didn't even— We had no chance to—" She collapsed into tears.

When the commotion died down, I hustled Cromwell out of the vicinity. I didn't know where to take him, and my shoulder hurt like hell, so I found a taxi stationed beyond the yacht basin and gave the driver the address of the cheap hotel where I'd been holing up for the past few days. The first thing I did when we were safely in my room was call Putnam and tell him to get up there with a doctor right away. The second thing I did was pour two stiff drinks for myself and Cromwell.

"Thank you, no. I never imbibe," he told me stiffly.

"It's for medicinal purposes," I assured him. "Go ahead. Drink it down."

"All right." He drank it and made a face. "I hope my wife Carrie doesn't find out about this," he said. "She's very active in temperance work."

I thought back to the last time I'd seen Carrie. She'd been lying stretched out naked on the bed at the Institute, the picture of the well-satisfied woman. There sure hadn't been anything temperate about her.

"Don't worry. I won't snitch," I promised Cromwell.

"In that case—" He held out his glass, and I refilled it. "It's just that Carrie's such a prude," he said apologetically as he downed it.

"I know just what you mean," I assured him soothingly.

"Wonderful wife, though. Takes an interest in my work. Takes an interest in my hobbies. My inventions. My campaigns to eradicate vice."

"Well, you and she will be back together again soon. Then you can go through life wiping out vice to your heart's content."

"Oh, I don't know. To tell the truth, it's too time-consuming. And sometimes Carrie can be too helpful. I mean, I wouldn't have gotten into this whole mess if she hadn't tried to help me by doing some investigating on her own."

"Well, maybe this cured her. Maybe—"

There was a knock at the door. Putnam entered. He had a small crowd with him. He took charge right away. Cromwell was hustled off by two of the men. They were taking him to the Pentagon where his "better mousetrap" alloy would be turned into a formula for a metal that would greatly expedite our space program. After they'd left, Putnam had the doctor set my shoulder.

"This man should go to the hospital," the doctor told him when he was finished.

"Not unless it's absolutely necessary," Putnam said. "He's needed here."

I looked at him in surprise, but I kept my mouth shut until after the doctor had left. Then I asked the question I'd been biting my tongue to hold back. "Why am I needed here?" I asked. "You've got Cromwell. The case is closed."

"Mr. Victor—Steve," he said, his tone becoming suspiciously friendly, "you are in an espionage position that offers the opportunity of a lifetime."

"What do you mean?"

"All you have to do is stay dead. On the way over here I received word over my car telephone that even now your 'widow' is making arrangements for your funeral. It's perfect. We even have a corpse. A corpse with your face. We won't even have to close the casket. We can bury Stevkovsky in your place, and you can take his place. What an opportunity. We can crack the entire Soviet espionage network with you in a position like that. What do you say?"

189

What could I say? I was hooked again. but I did insist on one privilege. "I want to go to the funeral," I told Putnam.

"What! But why?"

"It's the chance of a lifetime. How many men get to go to their own funerals? I wouldn't miss it for anything."

"But you're liable to be recognized."

"You can have your experts disguise me. And I'll stay at the back."

In the end, I got my way. But I was almost a little sorry I did. The crowd at the funeral chapel was disappointingly small. Still, Hortense looked so appealing in her widow's weeds, and she sobbed so loudly, that she almost made up for it.

Halfway through the ceremony Putnam nudged me and pointed to a bouquet of flowers. "I sent those," he whispered.

"That's a pretty small bunch," I griped.

"Well, you wouldn't have wanted me to be ostentatious, would you?"

"Cheapskate!"

After the chapel ceremony, we rode out to the graveyard. As the casket was lowered, Hortense tried to throw herself into the grave. She was saved by a United States senator who made a quick grab and latched onto her left breast.

"You must try to be brave, my dear," he said, showing no sign of relinquishing his hold.

"But I'm too young to be a widow," Hortense wailed. "Oh, my poor, darling Steve! It was bad enough for the wedding, but do you know I couldn't even find a Zoroastrian minister to preside at the funeral! Do you think he'd mind?"

I was all choked up. I wanted to tell her I didn't mind. But of course I couldn't. All I could do was watch myself being buried. After everybody else had left the side of the grave, I went up there all by myself. I wanted a moment alone with my grief. I dropped a handful of dirt onto the coffin.

"Good night, sweet prince," I murmured softly to myself. "Rest in peace, Steve Victor. Now, Man from O. R. G. Y., you belong to the ages."

I turned away from the grave and went back to Putnam. "What's the inscription on the headstone going to be?" I asked.

"How about 'My only regret is that I have but one life to give for my country'," he suggested.

"How wrong you are!" I told him. "How very wrong!"

And I proved it the next morning by starting out on my second double—double life, that is!

HAVE YOU MISSED
ANY OF TED MARK'S
SWINGING ADVENTURES?

THE MAN FROM O.R.G.Y.   72-918   50¢

Swing along with Steve "The Sex-Expert" Victor—
the unpredictable blend of James Bond, Casanova
and Dr. Kinsey. He's riding high in this remarkable
chronicle of spying and other racey goings-on.

**THE MAN FROM O.R.G.Y. returns in
THE 9-MONTH CAPER**   72-958   50¢

Still chasing spies and sex, Steve Victor goes Latin
and winds up in sizzling soup.

**THE MAN FROM O.R.G.Y. swings again in
THE REAL GONE GIRLS**   72-996   50¢

America's most unorthodox spy tackles an oddball
assignment: WOMAN-CHASING FOR A FEE!

THE GIRL FROM PUSSYCAT   73-446   60¢

She's a babydoll bombshell—looking for a match to
set her off. Penny Candie is her name and that's only
the beginning—her experiences are as riotous and
madcap as her handle.

THE NUDE WHO NEVER   72-989   50¢

How can a simple girl from the sticks, unskilled and
inexperienced make her way in the big city? To
Llona Mayper the answer was obvious—She was
young and naive—But man was she willing to learn!
The riotous results were not obvious at all.